A man sh... ...
years. A n... ...
meet agai...

Her heart was thudding with a tumult of feelings, emotions, memories. And slowly one question emerged. Why had he come back to haunt her? This was the man she had thought she loved—even, in those far-off days, thought she might marry. Until... Until...

She caught her breath in a sigh, a sob, and he looked directly at her. He didn't smile, and his voice was thoughtful.

'Hello, Jan,' he said. 'It's been a long time.'

From somewhere she found the strength to reply. 'Hello, Chris.'

Gill Sanderson, aka Roger Sanderson, started writing as a husband-and-wife team. At first Gill created the storyline, characters and background, asking Roger to help with the actual writing. But her job became more and more time-consuming and he took over all of the work. He loves it! Roger has written many Medical Romance™ books for Harlequin Mills & Boon®. Ideas come from three of his children—Helen is a midwife, Adam a health visitor, Mark a consultant oncologist. Weekdays are for work; weekends find Roger walking in the Lake District or Wales.

Recent titles by the same author:

TELL ME YOU LOVE ME
THE NOBLE DOCTOR
A CHILD TO CALL HER OWN
A VERY SPECIAL MIDWIFE

A NURSE WORTH WAITING FOR

BY
GILL SANDERSON

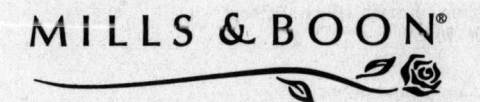

MILLS & BOON®

DID YOU PURCHASE THIS BOOK WITHOUT A COVER?

If you did, you should be aware it is **stolen property** as it was reported *unsold and destroyed* by a retailer. Neither the author nor the publisher has received any payment for this book.

All the characters in this book have no existence outside the imagination of the author, and have no relation whatsoever to anyone bearing the same name or names. They are not even distantly inspired by any individual known or unknown to the author, and all the incidents are pure invention.

All Rights Reserved including the right of reproduction in whole or in part in any form. This edition is published by arrangement with Harlequin Enterprises II B.V. The text of this publication or any part thereof may not be reproduced or transmitted in any form or by any means, electronic or mechanical, including photocopying, recording, storage in an information retrieval system, or otherwise, without the written permission of the publisher.

This book is sold subject to the condition that it shall not, by way of trade or otherwise, be lent, resold, hired out or otherwise circulated without the prior consent of the publisher in any form of binding or cover other than that in which it is published and without a similar condition including this condition being imposed on the subsequent purchaser.

MILLS & BOON and MILLS & BOON with the Rose Device are registered trademarks of the publisher.

First published in Great Britain 2006
Harlequin Mills & Boon Limited,
Eton House, 18-24 Paradise Road, Richmond, Surrey TW9 1SR

© Gill Sanderson 2006

ISBN 0 263 84742 X

Set in Times Roman 10½ on 12¾ pt
03-0706-50259

Printed and bound in Spain
by Litografia Rosés, S.A., Barcelona

CHAPTER ONE

IT COULDN'T be him! Please, no, it just wasn't possible!

Community Nurse Jan Fielding's summer holiday was ending with a bigger shock than she had ever thought possible. And whatever good the holiday had done her seemed instantly to drain away.

The call had come in the very early morning while she had been getting dressed. There had been that instant thrill of apprehension—early calls were often bad news.

It had been her boss, Dr John Garrett, calling, and his familiar voice had calmed her. 'Hi, Jan—have a good holiday? Come back fit and ready for work?'

'Both fit and ready, John. But why the early call? I'll see you in a couple of hours.' Now the thrill of apprehension was turning into a sense of excitement. This was an emergency call.

She glanced out her bedroom window as rain rattled on the glass. It might be summer but this was the Lake District. She guessed what was wrong. 'Don't tell me—you're turning out the mountain rescue team?'

'Sort of. I'm not turning out the full team, I don't think it's necessary. A couple of reasonably competent walkers have been stranded on the top of Yeaton Pike all night. They're experienced, they had bivouac equipment and they've just used a mobile phone to say they're on their way down. But the man seemed a bit doubtful about his wife. I told him to wait until someone meets them and leads them down Kelton Downfall.'

'Not a good place to be if you're tired and wet through,' Jan agreed. 'It can be treacherous in the wet. And there's that cliff edge nearby. So what do you want of me?'

'I want a couple of people to go up there, pick this couple up and escort them down. Walk in coils if necessary, just as a precaution. Are you up to it?'

Now, that was an insult. 'Of course I'm up to it. And I'll finish my normal day's work later. Who's coming with me? You?' John was leader of the Calbeck mountain rescue team.

His voice was hesitant. 'Not me this time. I'm getting a bit too old for it and, besides, I've twisted my ankle. Park at the head of Kelton Brook, there'll be someone there to go with you. He'll bring all the equipment you need. OK?'

'I'll be there. And I'll be in surgery later. Thanks, John.'

After ringing off she turned and looked at her blue community nurse's uniform laid out on the bed. Then she laughed, and reached in the cupboard for her climbing kit. She'd take her dress with her. Afterwards she could change in the surgery.

It was good to be back. As she drove her ancient Land Rover across country to the head of Kelton Brook she felt a deep content. After the brilliant blue of the Mediterranean sea and the dusty brown of the scrublands, the rain-soaked softer shades of the English Lake District seemed even more beautiful. She saw the peak of Sca Fell in the distance, half-hidden in mist. Yes, it was good to be back. She was ready to work among the people she knew and loved.

For two weeks she had luxuriated on the beach or at the poolside on a small Mediterranean island. She had picked a small, a quiet hotel. There was enough excitement in her life at home. Besides, she hadn't wanted to be up half the night drinking, dancing and carousing. Not any more. Not for years now.

She had enjoyed the local food and wine. She had wandered through a village or two, comparing the white-walled cottages with the grey stone of her own home. She had photographed olive groves and ancient buildings, tried out her guide-book Italian. But mostly she had just slept and read.

A couple men had invited her for a drink and she had automatically declined. The last thing she had been interested in had been a holiday romance. But she had quite enjoyed being asked. Perhaps she was now ready to start a proper life again.

But now she was home, rather proud of her carefully acquired tan, but more than happy to exchange her bikini for her wet-weather gear, and quite content that it was raining. She was home.

She drove to the head of Kelton Brook, stopped by a second Land Rover in a muddy field. Rain and mist swirled round her. She saw that the vehicle already parked was John's Land Rover—strange, he had said that he was not coming. He must have lent it to someone.

She could see a figure inside, who jumped out as she switched off her engine. The figure was taller than John; the hood of his blue anorak was up and his head was bent against the wind. Jan felt the first touch of anxiety. There was something she vaguely recognised about the figure—but she couldn't decide what. She knew all the other members of the rescue team, and it wasn't one of them. She didn't want to work with a stranger.

She felt more and more uneasy. Something was tugging at her memory. That walk?

Her passenger door opened, and the figure climbed in. He sat beside her, and pushed back his hood.

Then she knew why she had been apprehensive, as recognition came in a flash. She felt sick, clutching at the side of the door for support. This couldn't be happening to her, this wasn't possible!

Chris. Dr Chris Garrett. A man she hadn't seen for six years. A man she never wanted to meet again.

Her heart was thudding with a tumult of feelings, emotions, memories. And slowly, one question emerged. Why had he come back to haunt her? This had been the man she had thought she loved, even, in those far-off days, had thought she might marry. Until…until…

She caught her breath, in a sigh, a sob, and he looked directly at her. He didn't smile, and his voice was thoughtful. 'Hello, Jan,' he said. 'It's been a long time.'

From somewhere she found the strength to reply. 'Hello, Chris,' she said. 'It has been a long time. But not long enough.'

Somehow she managed to wrestle open her door, leaped out of the Land Rover and ran for the edge of the brook. One question hammered in her mind. What was Chris Garrett doing here?

She stopped and stared at the turmoil of waters, matching the turmoil of her own emotions. How could he come back? What did he want here? Had he come to torment her?

She heard the squelch of his boots in the mud, and he came and stood facing her. She lifted her head, stared at him.

He seemed bigger. Before he had been tall, broad-shouldered, but also what her father had described as whippet thin. Now he was heavier, but she could tell that the weight was muscle. Paradoxically, his face was thinner. There were lines down the sides of his cheeks, at the corners of his eyes. It was not the eager face of the young man she remembered. He looked older, like a man who had experienced more than he ought. But he still had the bluest of blue eyes.

At first nothing was said, and she was aware that he was studying her, too. Then he spoke and she shuddered as she heard that so-well-remembered voice.

'This is not the place I would have picked for a reunion,' he said. 'But we've got work to do. Can we put off any arguing till later?'

Her voice shook. 'I've got nothing to argue about with you. Anything I have to say I said six years ago.'

'Quite so. I remember it well. Now, are we going to the top of Kelton Downfall or not? I can manage without you if necessary.'

'Send you on a rescue on your own? You feel up to it? I think I'd better come along, just in case.'

She saw anger flicker in his eyes but he merely said, 'I've got the necessary kit in a couple of rucksacks in the back. Let's go.'

She followed him to the back of his Land Rover, and reached in to take the larger of the two rucksacks. He took it from her. 'You take the smaller one. I'm bigger than you, stronger, too. It'll be more efficient.'

She decided not to argue. But she led the way. Heads

down against the howling wind, they set off for the bottom of Kelton Downfall. Jan set a hard pace. She was young, fit and trained, and there weren't many people of either sex who could keep up with her. But Chris could. He stayed just behind her, slightly to one side.

They walked in silence for half a mile until they came to the bottom of Kelton Downfall.

The Downfall was a steep rocky slope, bordering a cliff edge. It didn't get much sun. The rocks were covered with lichen; when wet, they were a slippery deathtrap. But it was the quickest way down from the top of Yeaton Pike. Jan started the ascent.

Now she had to alter her pace a little: it was necessary to be safe. But a mean part of her wanted to know just how good Chris was, so she kept moving quickly.

After five minutes he caught up with her. 'If this is a competition, I suggest we keep it until there's only the two of us. Moving at this pace is dangerous. And right now we have patients to think of.'

He was right, of course, which only made her more angry, but she slowed down. And mysteriously they fell into a rhythm. He seemed as sure-footed as ever, his pace matching hers.

They could have made a good team.

In time they reached the top of the Downfall. Yeaton Pike was largely flat, and the wind tore across it, making even standing upright a difficult task. There was a little outcrop of rocks two hundred yards away. Chris lifted his arm, pointing, and Jan saw a flash of red there, obviously from an anorak. The couple were sheltering. That was good.

They were Paul and Dawn Kerrigan, a couple aged about forty. Jan looked approvingly at their kit: they were properly dressed, and obviously knew what they were doing. But Dawn looked pale.

'Sorry to put you to this trouble,' Paul said. 'It's good of you to turn out.'

That wasn't all that usual. Most people didn't realise that the mountain rescue team was all volunteers, working in their own time without any reward.

'No problem,' Chris said. 'Now, has either of you fallen? Any cuts, bruises, any aches that won't go away?'

'We've slipped a couple of times,' Paul said, 'but nothing serious.'

'How d'you feel? Cold? Miserable? Tired?'

Paul answered. 'I'm not too bad. I slept a little, Dawn didn't.'

Jan noticed that so far Paul had done all the talking. And what little she could see of Dawn's face was very pale.

Chris unslung his rucksack, and took out a Thermos and two mugs. 'There's something here to warm you up,' he said, 'but first I'd like to check your temperatures and then your pulse.'

Jan watched as he carried out a lightning check-up of the two. Then he turned and nodded curtly at her. Nothing apparently seriously wrong. 'You're easing towards hypothermia,' he told Dawn. 'You were right to send for us. We can get you down and then sorted out.'

'I'll take your rucksack,' Jan said.

Dawn shook her head and spoke for the first time, her voice low. 'You've got one already, and I...'

Chris took the rucksack from her. 'It'll be more efficient if Nurse Fielding takes it,' he said simply.

Dawn accepted this and Jan slipped the rucksack easily on top of her own. She'd carried far more than this, both while training and when operational.

They waited until Dawn and Paul had drunk the sugar-thick coffee and then headed for the top of the Downfall. There, Chris took the rope from round his shoulders, tied it round his waist, round the waists of Dawn and Paul and then Jan's. There was about twenty feet of slack between each person. 'You've walked in coils before?' he asked.

Paul answered. 'Only in snow, on a beginner's course in the Alps. Do we really need to here?'

'This can be as hazardous as any snowfield.'

The small party would walk close together, each holding much of the slack rope in coils in their hand. If one person were to fall the other three would act as an anchor. It was a simple but sometimes very effective precaution.

They set off down, Jan leading the way, Chris coming last. He was the strongest, the heaviest. Progress was necessarily slow. Dawn was tiring rapidly, and slipped three or four times. Once the rope pulled taut, though, she was in no real danger. Each time Chris was there, to help her to her feet, to assure himself that she was all right, to keep up her spirits by a couple cheerful remarks. And in time they reached the Land Rovers.

Chris helped them both into his Land Rover, and came to speak to Jan. 'I'll take them back to the surgery. I don't think it's necessary to send them to hospital, but I'll give them a quick check over and get them to rest.'

'Shouldn't your uncle look at them? After all, he is the doctor.'

'I'm a doctor, too, remember. And at the moment I'm the locum at the practice.'

'The locum! You mean you'll be working with me?'

'For a few months, yes.'

Jan swayed with the shock.

* * *

It was a half-hour drive to the surgery. Jan followed the other Land Rover and deliberately tried not to think about what had happened. Her calm, well-ordered life had been turned upside down, and this was something she didn't know how she could deal with. This was not the time to think, but she needed to know what had happened. Why was Chris back when he had said so forcefully that he never wanted to see her again? And she had never wanted to see him again either. It had been six years ago, but she still felt the same way. Why didn't he?

She couldn't, wouldn't think. She turned up the volume on her disc player and heard Ella Fitzgerald singing about the man she loved.

Great choice.

She wasn't needed to look after Dawn and Paul at the surgery—that was already in hand. So she shook hands, accepted their thanks and went to the changing room. The surgery was the meeting place of Calbeck Mountain Rescue Team, so there was provision for people to change and dry their wet clothes.

Jan showered, changed into her uniform, dried her hair. And slowly she gained control of herself. She was Jan Fielding, Community Nurse, working in one of the highest and hardest areas in England. She was known and respected; she could cope with anything. She would not cry. She would cope, as she always did. As she always had coped—almost.

She put on a touch of lipstick, straightened her uniform and her hair, and smiled at herself in the mirror—though there wasn't much to smile about. Now she was composed. And she felt a new emotion welling inside her. So far she had felt nothing but shock. Now she was feeling anger. How dared he show his face, come back to her home, her territory? She was going to find out and then make sure that everyone knew how she felt!

She marched out to do battle.

The door to the staff lounge was open and there were two men in it. Chris was there. He too had changed, presumably in the men's changing rooms, and was now smart in white shirt and dark trousers, not a mountaineer any more but every inch the doctor. The other man was the doctor in charge of the practice, her boss, John Garrett. He had been a family friend, known her parents. He had known her all her life, had encouraged her to become a nurse. Now he was stooped, moving more slowly. He was getting old, talking of retirement. She was sad about it.

But she still intended to take him to task when she had a chance. How could he have brought Chris back? Even if he was the younger man's uncle, he knew what she felt, knew what had been between Chris and herself.

The two hadn't yet noticed her. So she looked at Chris, the man she hadn't seen for six years. She knew she had changed—she was no longer a fresh-faced apprentice nurse. Her body, her face, her spirit had all matured. So how had Chris altered?

Then she saw him smile. Something John was saying was amusing him, and he smiled. It overwhelmed her with memories, and she felt something tugging at her inside, some kind of longing. And that reaction angered her even more.

She stepped forward, deliberately making herself heard, and the two men looked up. John looked as serene as ever, but there was a thoughtfulness in Chris's eyes.

'Well, you've worked together already,' John said, 'but perhaps it's time for more formal introductions. You remember Chris, my nephew, of course. He's been working in the floodplains of Bangladesh for the last six years. But now he's come home.'

'I remember him very well,' Jan said, unsmiling. 'How could I not?' She offered her hand to shake. 'What brings you back here, Dr Garrett?'

Chris was equally unsmiling. 'You know my uncle's trying to take things easier—that he's looking for a partner? Well, it's not going to be me. But I've offered to act as a locum for a couple of months, until he finds someone suitable.'

'So you don't intend to stay?'

He nodded at the mountains they could see out the window. 'The landscape doesn't suit me. I want something flatter. I thought Lincolnshire, or somewhere on the fens.'

'Is that so? Well, I hope you'll be happy in your short stay.'

'Happy?' He seemed to consider the idea as if it was new. 'We'll have to see about that.'

'Chris has started taking surgery for me,' John broke in, 'but he hasn't seen much of the district yet. Apparently the latest thing in general practice is for every new doctor to have an induction period—learn about procedures, protocols and so on.'

'Always a good idea to know what you're doing,' Jan said unkindly.

'Quite so. Well, I know he's been here before but if you don't mind, I'd like you to take him on your rounds today. I know you'll be wanting to see your regular patients. The locum nurse we hired was very good, but people round here want someone they know. Can you fit them all in this morning?'

Jan glanced at her watch and blinked. It was only an hour later than she normally started work. Of course, she had got up very early. 'I can fit them all in,' she said. Then she shot a glare at John, who appeared unruffled. 'Take Dr Garrett round with me?' she asked. 'Exactly why?'

'So he can get to know the area again and see some of our more distant patients. The people a doctor has to go out to see, because they have difficulty getting into the surgery. And I had a phone call from Mrs Thwaite at High Force Farm. She thinks her husband is getting worse, but he refuses to come down to see me. And I want a doctor to see him.'

'Fair enough,' Jan said reluctantly. 'I told you I wasn't happy with him. OK, I'll just check my messages and then get straight off. In, say, half an hour, Dr Garrett?'

He still didn't smile. 'Half an hour is fine,' he said. 'But I'd prefer it if you called me Chris. As you did before.'

'Call you Chris, as I did before,' she said. 'Well, why not? Call for me in half an hour, Chris.' And she left.

There was a lot of work to do before she could get out on her rounds. There were letters, e-mails, telephone messages, memos. She had to forget Chris for a while—though it was hard. She was still seething inside. How could he…? Work!

The nurse who had substituted for her had been fine. Jan had met her, had liked her. In the official diary she had listed the calls made, the medicines given. There were also a couple sticky notes attached—easy to take out and destroy. Often it was necessary to pass on information but not want it to be preserved in a semi-official form.

In fact, one note was about Herbert Thwaite, of High Force Farm. *Alzheimer's?* the nurse had pencilled. She was only a locum, the condition wasn't yet too serious and she obviously thought that a test and a decision about future treatment should be left to the regular team. But the couple of test questions she had asked had not been properly answered. *Unusually awkward and uncooperative. Wife not coping too well with the strain,* the note went on.

This was a problem Jan had seen coming. She sighed. Something would have to be done about Mr Thwaite—but it wasn't a nurse's job to decide.

The next note was even more worrying. Ben Mackie was a forty-year-old paraplegic—he had damaged his spine and was now confined to a wheelchair. In fact, Jan knew much of the blame was his: he had been drunk and driving his motorbike far too quickly. But Ben didn't accept it was his fault. It was the fault of the doctors, the nurses, the National Health Service, the country, his wife. Ben was bitter and made everyone's life a misery.

The nurse had noted: *Set of old and new bruises on face of Ben's twelve-year-old son. Boy says he fell over in yard. I doubt this. Query non-accidental injury?*

Jan sighed again. It wasn't her job to go looking for cases; she wasn't supposed to be a social worker. But, in fact, she often was. She kept an eye on people. If Ben was beating his son then something would have to be done by someone. She'd make a couple of discreet enquiries and then phone Social Services.

Jan made sure her case was full, checked that she had all the medicines that she would or might need. Her job was to visit the patients who couldn't—or sometimes wouldn't—come to the doctor's surgery. Much of her work was dealing with palliative care. She kept an eye on those who were on long-term medication. She visited the diabetics. A sad part of her work was visiting those with a terminal illness, who wanted their last days to be spent at home.

She glanced at her watch. Just a minute to go until half an

hour had passed—and almost to the second there was a tap on her door. She didn't shout *Come in,* but went to open it. Chris was there.

'Ready for me now?' he asked.

'Oh, I'm ready for you.'

The two of them walked out to her Land Rover. Typically, the rain had stopped and there was weak sunshine filtering through the clouds. She looked round, thrilled, as she always did when she saw what she thought of as *her* mountains. Then she glanced at Chris. He seemed less than thrilled: in fact, there was a definite frown on his face. This wasn't his ideal landscape.

But he looked well. He stood tall, seeming more confident than he had done when last she had seen him. And when he walked, she remembered the easy, long-legged stride that seemed so casual, and yet which ate up the miles. It was an odd reason for being first attracted to a man: because of the way he walked. But she remembered their very first meeting. She had seen him walking towards the surgery and—

What was she thinking? Suddenly she was angry at herself because she could remember, feel the attraction again. But it was long gone.

They reached her Land Rover and he frowned again when he saw the number plate for the first time. 'I remember this car when it was nearly new,' he said. 'It was…it was…' His voice trailed away.

'Yes, it was my father's car,' she told him. 'I kept it after he…after his death. Get in, it's unlocked.'

They set off with a jerk, but she didn't mind because she was blazingly angry. Yes, it was her father's car. So, yes, he did remember. She wondered what else he remembered, about her and about them…because she remembered every second of their time together. Even though she tried not to.

She was driving too fast. She took a corner and he was thrown against her, then she had to brake suddenly to let a sheep back scramble into its field. 'Do you always drive like this?' he asked calmly.

Only when angry was the answer, but she said nothing. She slowed down, though. No one else ought to suffer because of her bad temper.

After ten minutes they were well out of the village, heading up a narrow road towards the dalehead. She slowed then pulled off the road and sat for a moment, staring at the green-sided mountain ahead, hoping it would settle her turbulent feelings. Perhaps it did—a little. Chris sat silent, and she was glad of that.

After a while she said, 'We have to talk. I never expected—never wanted—to see you again. I thought you felt the same way. Why did you come back?'

He paused before replying. 'As a favour to my uncle,' he said. 'You know he's not well. He's desperately looking for someone suitable to be a partner, perhaps eventually to take over from him.'

'Yes, I know that,' she said. It calmed her a little, the thought that there were people with bigger problems than her. But still… 'So?'

'So he knew I was looking for a job and he wrote to ask if I would come and help for a while. Just till he got someone permanent.' Chris's voice was cold. 'I didn't want to come. There's nothing for me here.' He waved at the mountains. 'I hate this landscape, it oppresses me. I want somewhere flat. You can keep your mountains.'

For Jan this was near heresy but for the moment it was irrelevant. 'You could have said no,' she said. 'Pretended that you had a job lined up.'

'I could have. But John is my closest relation. Both my parents are dead.'

Out of the corner of her eye she saw him wince as he realised what he had said. She could have let him off, but she chose not to.

'Both my parents are dead, too,' she said. 'In fact, you were there when my father was fatally injured. Weren't you?'

There was silence in the car for a while and then she said, 'So don't you have bad memories when you come back here? Doesn't the past haunt you?'

'I do have some bad memories.' He frowned a moment, then went on, 'And, I must say, some good ones too. But the past doesn't haunt me. In the past six years I've seen so much pointless, unnecessary death that I think I've gone beyond being haunted. I've got used to it—or as used to it as you can be.'

'Well, I haven't got used to it. When I look at you I see the man who…the man who…'

She fell silent and the vision came back. She had it less often now. It used to come regularly, at night when she was overtired, or when she came across a forgotten photograph, or when she talked to someone.

Always the same. A dark, wind-howling night, the rain spattering down. Her father, lying on a stretcher, his face illuminated only by the light of the lamp fastened to her forehead. A great contusion on the side of his temple. And he was dead. When she glanced upwards there was Chris's face, wet, desperate and confused.

It was unusual to have the vision during the day. But when she did…

She stared across the fell, biting her lip to stop herself crying. But she knew that a couple tears were rolling down her cheeks.

'Sorry to cause you pain,' Chris said gruffly. 'But it won't be for long. Soon I'll be gone and I'll never come back. Don't let it worry you.'

'You'll never worry me,' she snapped. 'Now, we can work this out.'

She thought a moment, considering the days ahead, wincing at the prospect. Then she said, 'You'll only be here for a couple of months, and I can live with that misery for a while. Knowing that soon you'll be gone.'

'We can work together when we have to, but it won't be too often. I'll do my job in the surgery and other than that I'll see as little of you as possible. And then I'll be gone. Happy?'

'Very happy,' she said.

There was another silence and then she asked, in a more normal voice, 'Are you staying with John?'

He shook his head. 'No. I like to live on my own, I've got used to it. John's found me a cottage in Calbeck to rent.'

'Oh, I live in Calbeck, too. Where's your cottage?' She was struck by a horrible thought, and added anxiously, 'It's not that place at the end of Whiteside Lane?'

'I'm afraid it is.'

'Wonderful. We're neighbours. You're there at work during the day and just round the corner at night. But we can still keep apart.' She thought a moment and then went on, 'I suppose I'd better tell you. There are two pubs in Calbeck, the Bull and the Ensign Arms. I'm going to the Bull tonight, there's a little get-together there. A meeting of the mountain rescue team and its supporters. If you need a drink tonight I'd prefer it if you went to the Ensign.'

'I gather you're still a member of the mountain rescue team?' His voice was calm but she thought she could feel an edge to it.

'I certainly am. Nothing would stop me being a member. I love the work. Partly I do it in…memory of my father.'

'I see. Jan, my uncle isn't up to being the doctor of the team any more. You must have seen this coming. He's going to stay on as organiser—but for the present he's asked me to take his place when we go out on the fells. I've already been invited to meet the rest of the team at the Bull tonight.'

'You! You're the last thing we want!'

'The last thing the team wants or the last thing that you want?'

'They're the same. Your mountain rescue history isn't very good, is it?'

He sighed. 'Jan, it's six years since you met me. And in those six years I've done more emergency medicine than you've ever dreamed of. I've even trained in disaster medicine. The team needs me.'

She didn't reply because she knew he could be right. But where did that leave her?

The engine whined and rumbled as they bumped up the track to High Force Farm. It was halfway up the fellside, a tiny group of grey buildings, dwarfed by the sweep of the valley above and below. Today, in the weak sun, she thought it looked beautiful. But she knew it could be a hard and bitter place to earn a living.

Three people lived and worked here. There was Herbert Thwaite, his younger wife, Doris, and their son, Ken. They scratched a living farming sheep. It was a hard life—but they all loved it. And now Herbert was getting more and more cantankerous.

They bounced into the farmyard and parked. Jan listened to the engine a moment before turning it off, and shook her head gloomily. It didn't sound too healthy.

Doris had heard them arrive, and came out in her pinafore to greet them. She was obviously pleased to see them, and Jan noted just a touch of womanly reaction when Doris saw Chris. That irritated her.

'Good to see you back, Jan. We liked that other nurse but you know us all, don't you?'

'Certainly do,' Jan said cheerfully. 'I thought I'd drop in for a chat. This is Dr Garrett, by the way. Dr Chris Garrett.'

'Dr John's nephew?'

'That's right.'

'Oh, don't I remember? Didn't he…?' Doris obviously remembered then, and wisely decided that it would be a good thing not to say any more. 'Come on in,' she said instead. 'I'll pour you a mug of tea each. I put the kettle on as soon as I saw you coming up the track.' She led them into the farmhouse. 'Have you come to see Herbert, Dr Garrett?' Doris was obviously rather taken by Chris, Jan noted, stung once more.

'I'd like to have a word, if he's about. I gather you don't get out from here very much?'

'No. Ken does most of the shopping at the weekends. He likes to go into town to stay the night with his mates. Now, I'll just go and make Herbert ready.' Doris hurried out of the room.

Jane felt a bit guilty. She had been so concerned with her

own feelings that she had not been properly professional. She should have briefed Chris before. Now she muttered, 'Herbert is seventy-six. He's worked all his life on the fells—he inherited this farm from his father. About three years ago he had a fall, broke his hip. So now he can't get about as much as he used to and he frets a lot. When he was younger he used to be a fell-runner. The locum nurse feels he might have incipient Alzheimer's.'

Chris nodded. 'Can we get him to see a consultant?'

Jan sighed. 'He won't come down to hospital. He hated it when he was in three years ago.'

'We'll just have to see. How's Doris?'

'Doris is a tough one and she loves Herbert. She's younger, of course. She'll cope.'

'I'm sure she will. But I'd like to have a look at her. Just to check her over.'

'Why? Any special reason?'

'No special reason—but why not?'

Doris came back and invited them into the bedroom. Chris examined Herbert, then he gave him the standard mini-mental test. Jan winced as she listened to Herbert's fumbling answers. He wasn't sure of the time or place, he scored poorly on simple memory tests, he couldn't concentrate. Definite cognitive impairment.

And Herbert was generally awkward. 'Why can't John Garrett come out? I don't want to be messed around by a young kid like you.'

'John's not as young as he used to be,' Chris replied. 'But he asked me in person to say hello. Now, what's this about you used to be a fell-runner in your younger days? I used to do a bit of running myself...'

And that started Herbert. Chris could now do what he liked.

Reluctantly, Jan had to admit to herself that Chris was a good doctor. His examination was thorough but unobtrusive and he kept Herbert happily talking. When he said that he'd be back again, Herbert grudgingly said that he'd be pleased to see him. Then they went back downstairs.

'You were good with him, Dr Garrett,' Doris said. 'I know he can be a bit awkward at times—but you calmed him properly.'

'I'm afraid we'll have to be back soon,' Chris said. 'I'm not very happy about his mental condition—but there are a lot of things we can try. How are you, Mrs Thwaite? How d'you feel?'

The question seemed to confuse Doris. 'I'm fine. I get a bit tired at times, but we all do, don't we?'

'How long since you had an examination?'

'I don't need an examination. I've no time to be ill.'

'Well, I'd like to take a look at you. And Jan here thinks it would be a good idea.'

'It certainly couldn't hurt,' Jan said.

This time they went to the spare bedroom. The examination didn't take long—and then Chris asked Jan to take a blood sample. He said that they'd be in touch very soon, and the pair of them left.

Jan was quiet as they bounced back down the track. But when they reached the road, and driving didn't take so much of her attention, she started to wonder. Had she missed something with Doris? It was part of her job to watch out for signs of illness in her patients, signs that might not always be obvious. She didn't know whether to feel anxious or irritated.

'What were you looking for in Doris?' she asked after a while. 'Was there anything specific?'

He shrugged. 'Nothing too specific. Is she a bit more exophthalmic than she used to be?'

Jan thought. 'Possibly,' she said. 'But you tend not to notice behind those glasses she wears.'

'True. Her eyes could protrude a lot more before it was obvious. Did you notice her neck?'

'Yes. Normally she wears high-necked sweaters—but there was some swelling there.'

'Possibly a goitre. I wondered if she might be developing hyperthyroidism. Has she got more anxious recently—when you call, is she always running round, trying to get things right? And was she always that way?'

Jan thought. 'Her behaviour has changed a bit recently,' she said. 'But I thought it was just worry about Herbert.'

'It still might be that. Have you any details of her family? Are any of them hyperthyroid—do they have Graves's disease?'

'I don't know. But I can find out. I'll ask John. And then the one who knows most about the district is probably Penny Driscoll. Remember…'

As her voice tailed away, Jan cursed herself. She didn't want to go back to how things had been before. The best thing to do would be to put the past behind her.

Penny Driscoll had been the community nurse before her, and she knew everyone and everything in the valley. When Jan had first met Chris she had been shadowing the older woman, going out on her rounds with her. She had learned so much.

'I remember Community Nurse Penny Driscoll very well,' Chris said. 'A very competent woman. But she must have retired by now.'

'She has. But her mind is still as sharp as it ever was and she knows about everyone in the valley. I'll ask her about Doris.'

'Is she keeping well?'

'Very well. I call on her quite often, she lives about ten miles away.'

'I'd like to meet her again.'

'I'll give you her address,' said Jan. No way was she going to take him with her. 'What are we going to do about Doris?'

'See what results we get from the lab. If it is Graves's disease, we can start her on antithyroid drugs for a while. Then there's always the possibility of partial thyroidectomy, or even radioactive iodine therapy. But they're well in the future.'

'Quite,' said Jan. She was annoyed. She was the community nurse—she should have spotted what was wrong. She was glad Chris didn't say so. She decided to talk about something else.

'Now, most of the next calls aren't so far in the hills. First is Melanie Thomas. She's a diabetic, she's eighty-one and as sharp as a needle. She lives alone and I just call on her a couple of times a month to make sure she's sticking to her diet and her treatment.'

'Nothing specifically wrong with her at the moment?'

'I doubt it. But with old people, catch something early and you stand a much better chance of dealing with it. And Melanie makes a wonderful cup of tea.'

As ever, Melanie was thriving. But she did ask Chris if he'd like to call again some time.

They called on Jack Lewis after that. Jack had terminal mesothelioma of the lungs. The cancer was a complication of asbestosis: Jack had been a quarryman and had been over-exposed to brown asbestos dust. John Garrett had put him in touch with a lawyer and there was hope of compensation. Not that that was any consolation to his family.

'The family is close, they want him to die at home,' Jan explained. 'They know that nothing further can be done—they've accepted that.'

'So what treatment is he getting?'

'Just painkillers. Morphine from a syringe driver. He's only half-conscious now—I call to see his family as much as I call to see him. Most of the time they need a friend, not a nurse.'

'It's good when you can be both,' he said.

The visit to Ben Mackie wasn't as unpleasant as it usually was, possibly because of Chris's presence. Ben felt he could bully women—or he could try. Chris's silent presence unnerved him a little.

Jan checked Ben for any signs of deterioration and warned him once again of the danger of bed sores.

'Only you can prevent them, Mr Mackie. Keep yourself clean and dry, and if there's the slightest sign of reddening of the skin, use the barrier cream I gave you.'

His voice was half angry, half self-pitying. 'Didn't do any good. Look at this mess, it's going red already. Who's responsible for this?' Mr Mackie pointed to one of his elbows.

'You can deal with your elbows yourself, Mr Mackie. The remedy is in your own hands.'

This time there was no attempt at making friends, no extra effort to try to put the patient at ease. Jan had tried, and had been insulted for her pains. Now she remained professional, civil—but that was all.

'Haven't seen your son for a while Mr Mackie,' Jan said, just before they were about to go. 'Is he around anywhere?'

'Why d'you want to know?'

'I heard that apparently he had a nasty fall. Hurt his face. I just wanted to check he was all right.'

'He's at school. Where he ought to be.' Well, that was that. Technically, she couldn't get in touch with Social Services until she had seen the bruises herself. But she half suspected that the locum nurse had been right. What she could do was ring the school. She had friends there.

At the end of a round trip of about four hours, they headed back for the surgery. In spite of herself, Jan had to admit that Chris was a good doctor. He didn't intrude, he let her get on with her work. He chatted happily to most of her patients. When she asked his opinion, or suggested he might like to examine someone, he made sure that she was part of the process. He saw the two of them as a team, not two individuals with differing skills. And she had to admit, she liked that. The morning hadn't gone as badly as she had feared. Whatever her personal feelings, they could be professional together.

They had to drive over one of the smaller passes and climb up to a high point before dropping down into their own valley. Jan stopped at the top, pulled off the road and cut the engine. Never mind what Chris thought, she always did this. The view was tremendous.

She just couldn't help herself. 'Look at that! Isn't it wonderful?'

He glanced through the windscreen. 'I told you, I prefer flat land.'

'But before, you used to—'

He cut in. 'I *used to* do a lot of things. But I'm not the boy I was then. I've changed.'

His voice was cold again. For the first time she realised that he might feel as bad about her as she felt about him. It was a new, interesting, upsetting idea. He was the guilty one! Their parting had been about what she felt, not about what he felt.

'Fine,' she said. 'I'll not mention it again.'

Time to go. She turned on the ignition. Nothing happened. She waited a few seconds and then tried again. Still no result. This couldn't be happening to her, not here, not now! But it had happened before. Her Land Rover was getting old and temperamental.

She turned to Chris, the man she'd ignored for the past few minutes. 'I'm afraid we've broken down,' she said.

It struck her as an apt thing to say.

CHAPTER TWO

SHE wouldn't give up. Viciously Jan turned the key another three or four times, each time without a result. Finally Chris said, 'You're only running down the battery. May I try?'

'It won't start just because you're a man,' she snarled. 'But suit yourself.' She climbed out of the driver's seat, left the door open and went to look at the view. If it *does* start for him, she thought, as soon as I get back, I'll kick it.

She glanced at him as he slid into her seat, turned the key—and appeared to listen. 'This has happened before,' he said, telling her rather than asking. 'You should have it fixed.'

'True. Thanks for that valuable piece of advice.'

She saw him reach down, heard the thump as he undid the bonnet catch. Then he leaned over to pick up his doctor's bag and took out a pair of rubber gloves.

Rubber gloves? 'Are you going to operate on the engine?' she asked. 'Do you need an anaesthetist and a scrub nurse?'

He didn't react to her sarcasm, just shook his head and said, 'It's not a really good idea to move from engine to patient. Patients get upset if they see black oily hands on the doctor.'

'I see. And are you a mechanic as well as a doctor?'

He shrugged. 'I drove for months in Bangladesh in a Land Rover, it's a popular vehicle. And out there you're often miles from the nearest mechanic, so if anything goes wrong, you quickly learn to fix it yourself. Or you just don't move. So I got to be quite a proficient mechanic. Have you got a tool kit?'

'There's one in the back, but I don't know what's in it.'

As he moved to the back of the vehicle, she sighed. This man was getting to be too much for her. And then another thing struck her. The Chris she remembered had been much easier to anger. Not for a moment would he have put up with the insults she had just directed at him. This man was calm, or he had learned to discipline himself—she didn't know which. Whatever, she felt that he had put her at a disadvantage.

He took off his jacket, rolled up his shirtsleeves and leaned over the engine. She could see the tautness of his trousers over the well-shaped thighs, see the muscles of his back. He had a beautifully proportioned body. She had rarely seen a man who was so…

She didn't need this! This was a man she disliked intensely, a man who had ruined her life. So what if he was now a gorgeous specimen of manhood? It was what was inside that counted.

She heard the tinkle of a spanner, heard a grunt of satisfaction. When she turned she saw his engrossed face. It was a look she remembered. He was an enthusiast in all he did, it was something she had loved about him. If they were talking about some aspect of medicine, he wanted to know everything. A quick, easy answer was not enough.

There was a sudden flash of memory, and she turned away

from him. Six years before, a holidaymaker, a camper, had been brought to the surgery by his wife. He had been complaining of stomach cramps and vomiting. The first, most likely diagnosis had been that he'd had some kind of food poisoning. But after questioning it had turned out that earlier that day he had picked some wild mushrooms and eaten them. His wife hadn't eaten any. No, he couldn't remember exactly what they looked like. John had sighed and sent him off to hospital. His diagnosis had been confirmed later: the man had been suffering from muscarine poisoning—he'd picked the wrong mushroom. But he hadn't eaten the most deadly of mushrooms, *Amanita phalloides,* and he'd survived.

John had talked to them both afterwards, explaining the symptoms and treatment of fungus poisoning. Chris had listened, fascinated. He had sat up half the night reading about the condition and memorising every picture of a poisonous mushroom, then had spent much of next day telling her what he had learned. She had loved him for it. She had loved him then for his enthusiasm.

Angry with herself again, she looked round. As ever, there was peace to be found in the landscape. As her eyes dwelled on the rocks, the greenness of the grass, the sharp-edged cliffs, slowly she felt serene again. With this around her, life couldn't be all bad.

Behind her there was a rumble. The Land Rover's engine. She turned. 'How did you manage that?' she asked. 'What was wrong?'

'It was a fuel-pump problem. That's what I was listening for when I turned the key; you get a ticking if the pump is working. No ticking, no fuel getting through. So I swapped the windscreen-wiper fuse with the fuel-pump fuse—and there we were, in business. But the wipers won't work now. Buy a fuse for them and I'll fit it. A reward for driving me around.'

'Of course,' she said.

He turned to have a last critical look at the engine, before slamming down the bonnet. 'Another thing, Jan, this engine is old and tired. It needs a major service. And I didn't like the way the brakes squealed and jerked when we were coming down that hill. You'd better put this in and get an estimate.'

'And that will cost?'

'I'm afraid that it'll cost plenty,' he said.

'I'll see that it's done,' she said gloomily.

She had overspent on her holiday and was not happy at the thought of further major expense. Still, it had to be done.

They climbed into the car, and she set off for the surgery. A thought came, unbidden, and before she could stop herself, she spoke. 'You didn't use to be mechanically minded. You weren't interested. Not unless it was an X-ray machine or something.'

'I'm a different man now.'

That afternoon Chris went off with John and she worked on her own. She had a well-woman clinic at the surgery. It was work she enjoyed and helped her keep in touch with the community. She ran the cervical smear test programme and there had been three cases when she'd had to send an unsuspecting woman to the doctor for a fuller examination. Two early stage cancers detected, both treatable because they had been caught early. It made her feel good.

And there was the never-ending gossip. Well, why not?

'I hear we've got a new doctor,' teenager Alice Plows said after Jan had finished taking her blood pressure. 'He's only recently come to the village. I've just seen him, he looked gorgeous. Don't you fancy him, Jan?'

'No, I don't,' Jan said firmly. 'And, in fact, I can't. The last thing you want in a job is complications like that. Don't mix work and relationships, Alice. Now, how do you like your new job at the post office? Getting on with everyone there?'

'It's a great job, and everyone's been really helpful.' There was a small reddening on Alice's cheeks. 'And Mr Henshaw is really nice.'

The local post office, general store and camping-kit shop was run by father and son Keith and Joe Henshaw. Jan knew them both.

'Really nice? That'll be Joe Henshaw.'

'Yes, Joe,' Alice said, reddening even more. 'In fact…he's taking me for a drink at the Bull tonight.'

'I'm going to be there myself,' said Jan. 'Got a meeting.'

'Is it really bad to mix work and relationships, Jan?'

'Well, it can work for some people. If they're careful.' And that was as far as Jan intended to go about relationships.

But there was one thing more—and she had to be delicate about it. 'If you and Joe—or any man for that matter—get to be close, before you—'

'Are you talking about birth control?'

'Yes,' said a relieved Jan.

'Not necessary yet, but it might be soon and when it is I'll come to see you. I know you'll be able to help me.'

'Right,' said Jan.

She was so busy, she managed to forget Chris until nearly the end of her day. She was about to go home when she saw John. At first she felt a bit guilty—John looked a little more bent, a little more tired than usual. And he was limping: his ankle must be paining him. But still she had things to say to him that couldn't wait. 'Chris gone?' she asked.

'Yes, he's gone home. Did you want him?'

'Not at all. I wanted you. Could we have a word, please, John?'

'I've been expecting this. You'd better come into my room.'

She followed him, sat in the chair by the side of his desk and for a moment both were silent.

She thought John was looking more tired than ever. There was a greyish tint to his skin, and she could hear his heavy breathing. They had been friends a long time, and she didn't want to add to his worries. But still...he had caused her some worries.

'I haven't asked you if you had a good holiday,' he said. 'Did you?'

'It was all right. In fact, it was more than all right. I had a good time.'

'Do anything exciting? Meet anyone new?'

'I don't want to be excited or to meet anyone at all,' she said. 'John, can we get down to business?'

He looked at her in an appraising way that made her feel rather uncomfortable. But he merely said, 'Of course. And I suspect I know what you're going to say.'

Perhaps he did know. But knowing what she was going to say wasn't going to stop her saying it. 'Working with Chris is going to be hard for me,' she said. 'I'm not sure that I can cope. You know our history, so why did you do it, John? Why did you bring him here? And don't tell me you just needed a locum, we've managed well enough so far and you'll have a new partner soon. So why cause me this pain? Didn't you know how it would affect me? It's just not like you.'

There was silence for a moment and then he said, 'I had to do quite a bit of persuading. Chris didn't want to come. He said that anything that he could offer here, or anything that here could offer him, was over.'

'I feel the same way,' Jan said.

'And I didn't want him back in Bangladesh. He's done his bit there.'

'I can see that. But why here?'

John paused a moment and then said, 'Because I think there's unfinished business between you two. I know what pulled you apart, but that was six years ago. And neither of you has recovered. You're not who you were. This will give you a chance to sort out your problems.'

She couldn't believe what she was hearing. 'John, you're interfering! It's just…just not you! I've got nothing to say to Chris, he's got nothing to say to me. Everything was said six years ago. John, it's over!'

'If it's over, you should have no problem working together,' John said calmly. 'And it's only for a couple of months. But neither of you has been in any kind of lasting relationship, and I wondered—'

'I was engaged to Peter Harris!'

'So you were. And…?'

'It was just that he wasn't the man for me. We parted by mutual consent.'

'I'm not surprised. Jan, what happened between you and Chris was six years ago. And neither of you has got closure. It's still festering inside both of you. This is your chance to get things sorted out. Or are you going to wander through life with the burden getting heavier all the time?'

She stood, more angry than she could ever remember with

this man. 'You're wrong, John. For the first time since I've known you, you're absolutely and utterly wrong. I'll put up with these two months, I'll work with the man. But don't you ever interfere with my life again in this way!'

She slammed out of the room.

It was a tiny cottage that John had found for Chris, but he thought it was luxurious. It came fully equipped with bedding, cutlery, crockery—all he needed to provide was his own clothes and personal effects. And he didn't have many of those.

Over the last six years he had wandered about, staying and sleeping in the strangest of places. For him the old saying was true—home was where you hung your hat. He had hardly made any impression on the living room at all. There were no pictures, no photographs no ornaments. Just his computer and a shelf of books—all of them medical textbooks. It would take him an hour to move out. That was how he liked it.

He came in that evening, changed out of his formal clothes and cooked himself a meal. Rice, lentils, a vegetable curry, then fruit. A diet he'd got used to. Then he sat in the single armchair and decided he wouldn't have a drink as he was going to the Bull later. And so he thought about his day.

Meeting Jan again, treating her as if she were just an old acquaintance, had been hard, though not as hard as he had expected. There had been none of the anticipated rush of anger. But he had certainly been disturbed by her.

He hadn't seen her for six years. When he had first gone abroad he had thought about her constantly. He'd tried to banish the memory, and slowly it had grown less and less. But it had never disappeared. And sometimes still, even after six years, often when he was tired, she would appear in his memory. Leaving him angry—or sad.

It had been a shock to realise just how much she had changed. He remembered a nineteen-year-old girl, youthful, eager, often a bit unsure of herself. This new Jan was different. She was a woman, with a woman's poise and dignity. She was assured, certain of her own skills, quietly aware of her own abilities. But the bubbling brightness had gone.

Physically she had changed, too. Her body had filled out slightly; she was no longer gangly but slim, with more mature curves. He remembered her with long hair, held back with a coloured ribbon. Now it was short. Efficient, he supposed, but he preferred it as it had been.

Her face was as breathtakingly lovely as ever. But perhaps there was a reserve in those large grey eyes, and when she smiled she was not as giving as before.

It had hurt him when he had seen her for the first time, the shock had been so great. What had been said and done still caused pain. But there was another feeling that he could not quite identify. There was sadness that something that had been wonderful had passed. It *had* passed, of course, it could never be retrieved. But still…it was a pity.

It was odd to find her here, still in a world that mysteriously seemed not to have changed very much. His life had been different—hard, tiring, usually lonely, occasionally dangerous. He could feel the attraction of this kind of life. He'd find a job as a country GP—there were plenty advertised. Perhaps somewhere in Lincolnshire or the Fens. But not here in the Lake District. Mountains still filled him with a sense of foreboding. Mountains made him think of Jan.

Time for him to move if he was going to the meeting at

the Bull. He looked out of the window. It was raining. 'Typical Lakeland weather,' he murmured to himself, and then remembered that the phrase had been a joke between Jan and him. He had once looked out when it had been raining and said, 'Typical Lakeland weather.' After that, every time the sun shone she had shouted, 'Typical Lakeland weather!' A daft joke, but it had amused them. They had been so—

Time to go!

No point in getting wet—he'd drive. It only took him a moment to change and then he set off, wondering if this was the right thing to do, deliberately getting so close to Jan. He didn't need to be a member of the rescue team; he could back out even though he knew that his uncle wanted him to do the job. But it might be the kinder thing for Jan if he resigned. Then he realised. He wanted to see more of Jan.

Just curiosity, he told himself.

He had been to the Bull before, and liked the place. He entered by the side door, quietly ordering himself a half pint of bitter. He didn't want to be seen at once, preferring to observe a little.

He saw her but she didn't see him. She was sitting with a group around a table, laughing and joking, obviously at home with everyone. He stood in a quiet corner, and he watched.

Jan had looked so good in the nurse's uniform. But now she looked even better. She was wearing a burgundy sleeveless dress, a colour that contrasted with her eyes. And as he watched, he felt the same reaction that he had felt six years before when he had first seen her. A heart-stopping attraction.

Jan loved working with the Calbeck Mountain Rescue Team. Like the others in the Lake District, it was manned entirely by volunteers. It wasn't as big as some of the others. But they trained, were efficient. They had carried out several rescues that otherwise might have had dangerous, even lethal consequences. It felt good to be part of them.

She walked into the Bull, waving, and shouted greetings to her friends. She felt at home. There was Alice, the girl she had spoken to that afternoon, sitting with the man who was technically her employer, Joe Henshaw. They were sitting very close to each other and seemed to be getting on well. Alice saw her looking, waved and blushed. Seems quite serious, Jan thought.

She walked to the table where the group was sitting and took a seat between two of them. It was good to be back among friends. She caught up on the gossip, showed her newly tanned arms, told them that Italian wine wasn't half as good as British beer. Then she looked up and there in the corner was Chris. They made eye contact, and he lifted his glass in salutation.

It was just that she hadn't expected to see him there, she told herself. Her heart lurched—but whether in surprise or anger, she didn't know. Or perhaps it was something else.

He had changed out of the semi-professional clothes he had been wearing earlier, was now in chinos and a white T-shirt. It was the most difficult of outfits for a man to wear—every bodily flaw showed—but Chris looked good in it. He was solid muscle, no sign of fat.

She knew it had to be done and she was the best person to do it. So she walked over to Chris and said, 'You'd better come and meet the rest of the group. You'll be working with them.'

'Sounds like a good idea.'

There were a dozen or so people around the table. Jan introduced Chris to them as the locum doctor and explained that John Garrett felt that, although he'd continue to support the group, he didn't feel up to climbing mountains any more. If the group was willing, Chris would take his place for a while.

'I've done a bit of work on these mountains,' Chris said. 'But I'm nowhere near as expert as any of you. I'm happy to be led. But I've had considerable experience with emergency medicine and that's where I might be of some use.'

There was a murmur of approval at that. And if there was to be an interview, Chris had just passed it.

Then Jan realised something. There were two people there who had been members of the team six years ago. She was one. The other was Perry Sheldon, a local hospital administrator, who was usually the group's leader.

'Chris Garrett?' he said thoughtfully. 'Weren't you here some time ago? Didn't you have something to do with...?' Then his voice trailed away as he remembered.

Jan could see Chris whitening. Quickly, she said, 'Chris was on the rescue when my father died. Now, please, can we talk about something else?'

She knew that her voice had been loud, shrill, but she couldn't help it. Quickly Perry said, 'It was a long time ago,' and changed the subject And for a while that was fine.

The little group carried on with its business as usual. There was the talk about equipment, about funding, about liaison with the police. Chris listened but said little, which was a good thing. And then it was finished. Like all their meetings, a casual but an effective one. And Chris was going to be accepted. Jan wasn't sure what she felt about that.

Most of the members drifted home. Perry talked to Chris

about Bangladesh. And Jan yawned. It had been a long and emotionally tiring day.

Quietly, Chris said, 'It's raining and I didn't see your car outside. Would you like me to drive you home? After all, we are close neighbours.'

'I'll be fine walking, thank you. I have my anorak.'

'It is very wet, and you've had a hard day. You're not afraid of getting in the car with me, are you?'

Now, that was a challenge. 'No, I am not. All right. You can give me a lift.'

It was hard maintaining the appearance of friendliness with him. But she knew she had to. The rescue team was a tightly bonded group, any friction between its members would result in inefficiency. She did not want to pull the group apart.

So she got in his car—a small hired one, she noticed—and he drove her home. He made no attempt to speak to her, and after a while she found it irritating.

'Are you looking forward to working with the group?' she asked.

His voice was laconic. 'I am. They seem very friendly. Most of them.'

'You can't expect me to be your friend!'

'I don't. But we can work together.'

'Right.' Then there was silence until he pulled up outside her cottage. 'Thank you for the lift,' she said tautly. 'And that, I think, takes care of everything we have to discuss. Good night.' And she was out of the car, dashing down her path to the front door.

She noticed that he waited until she was inside before he drove off. She locked the door behind her—and for what seemed like the tenth time that evening gave a great sigh.

Her head was whirling. It had been an eventful day.

* * *

Jan calmed herself by walking around her home. It was her treasure, her delight. She had sold the farmhouse where she had lived with her father—her memories had made it too much for her to live there on her own—and she had bought this place, spending a lot of money on having it converted. And now, though she said so herself, it was a little gem.

On the ground floor, three tiny rooms had been converted into one long one. The plaster ceiling had been stripped to reveal the two-hundred-year-old beams. A brand new kitchen had been built onto the rear. Upstairs there were three bedrooms, one for herself, one as spare and one used as her study. There were two bathrooms.

She had picked her own decor, her own pictures and ornaments. This was her home and her refuge. Whenever she walked in, she felt an instant sense of welcome, of being at ease.

She had a long luxurious bath. Then she moisturised her face, pulled on her robe and went downstairs to sit by the fireplace with her cocoa. She used her remote to click on her DVD player, and had to smile. The music started softly at first. It was Aretha Franklin singing 'I Will Survive'.

Will I survive? Jan thought. Then, What have I got to survive?

It was three days before they had to go out on the mountains together.

It was early evening and she had just left the surgery. She was almost glad when her phone rang and John called her out on a rescue. 'A party of three on Leffkow Rise—a man and two younger boys. Rang in on the man's mobile phone. It's not life-endangering, they seem to have adequate kit and they're keeping warm. The man has a damaged ankle that sounds as if it is very badly sprained. And when he fell he hit his head—a fair amount of blood but he thinks it's only a cut.'

'Never trust a man who diagnoses himself,' said Jan. It was a mantra drilled into her by Penny.

She put on her kit and drove back to the surgery. Now she would have to go out with Chris and the group. It would be a relief to find out that she could manage it.

She arrived at the surgery, the meeting point for the rescue members, where their kit was stored. The other members arrived shortly after her. Chris was there, looking efficient in his climbing gear, but he didn't speak much to her. Instead, he seemed to be getting to know the other members of the group. She was glad.

They set off in two Land Rovers, one man co-ordinating, keeping in touch with the police. They all knew the area and drove as far as possible up to the valley head. Then they parked and each picked up the rucksack with the allocated kit.

Perry told them what he thought was the best route to the summit. Jan suggested another one—longer but, she thought, faster. After a moment's thought, Perry nodded. They would take her route. The rescue party set off.

Jan was almost enjoying herself. Here they were, eight people, different ages and trades, but united in skill and a desire to help. Only Chris posed a possible problem, and he kept away from her. This made a change from her normal nursing work. She was a good walker, and had no trouble in keeping up with the others—who were all men. They moved on steadily, their regular pace eating up the distance.

No one talked. They needed their energy to keep moving, and this Jan enjoyed, too. It gave her time to look round, to enjoy the gradually unfolding views. And she couldn't help herself. Casually, she kept glancing at Chris. He moved well, looking as efficient as the others. Then she remembered the time six years ago when they had been on a rescue together—and the pain was greater than ever.

The party was now at the beginning of Leffkow Rise. High ahead they saw the orange of an anorak and someone waved at them. Presumably the party they had come to rescue. It was easy to see how an accident could happen here. The ground was littered with loose stones, and the wind blew in sudden sharp gusts—enough to make someone lose their footing. Jan and the rest of the party slowed a little—the last thing they needed was one of their own injured.

Chris was the doctor, so he went straight to the injured older man. But he started his examination only when she was by his side. Reluctantly she had to admire him for that: too many doctors thought that they alone had the right to diagnose. Chris intended to include her.

The man's ankle was obviously badly sprained. 'Name's Barry Houghton,' he said, as the two bent over him. 'Sorry to put you to this trouble—but I have the two boys with me and I didn't dare put them at risk.'

'You did the right thing,' Jan said. 'We'd rather be called out now than when things were really desperate. Who are the boys?'

'Les and Eric. I don't know them well. A friend of mine who runs a club asked me to give them some idea of what mountain walking was like. Suspect they won't be too keen after this.'

'Don't bet on that,' said Jan.

Chris asked Jan to strap up the ankle. This was nurse's work. Then Barry said he thought he could walk. Both Chris and Jan shook their heads. He would be carried down.

They looked at the wound on Barry's head. It had bled, but looked to be only a surface scratch. Barry was certain that he had not lost consciousness, not even for a moment. The pupils of his eyes were the same size. The two decided there were no signs of concussion and Jan put a temporary dressing on the wound.

Now they turned to the two young lads, aged twelve and thirteen. Both had obeyed Barry's instructions, had kept warm and not wandered. They were a little frightened but all right and assured Jan that they hadn't fallen, they had no problems whatsoever.

Jan thought the older lad seemed a little hesitant. His answers were slow, and she wanted to talk to him longer. But Perry was insisting that they set off. It might come on to rain. Barry was strapped into the portable Bell stretcher, and they would stick to the usual system of alternating carriers. Jan was given the job of keeping her eye on the two young boys.

For a while all went well. Then Jan noticed that, even though their pace was slowed by the fact they had to carry the stretcher, she and the two lads were lagging behind. It was Les, the older boy, who was slowing the pace.

'Chris,' she shouted, 'hold it for five minutes. And can you come here, please?'

Chris did as she asked. 'It's easy walking and it's downhill,' he said to the two boys. 'I would have thought that two strapping lads like you would have no trouble. Is there any pain at all?'

Both shook their heads.

Suddenly, Jan guessed. She sighed and took Les to one side. 'How long since you ate?' she asked.

Les looked at her as if he couldn't understand the question.

'You're diabetic, aren't you?' Jan asked. 'At a guess, type two. And you've missed a meal because you were stranded on a mountaintop?'

Les managed to nod.

'I've got just the thing for you.' Jan took off her rucksack, and pulled out a bottle of excessively sweetened orange juice. 'Drink this.'

Les did as he was told. And then he was ready to carry on walking almost at once. Jan always marvelled at the speed with which a hypoglycaemic patient would recover when given sugar.

'Didn't Mr Houghton know you were diabetic?' Jan asked. 'Didn't he know that you needed special care?'

Les looked shamefaced. 'I didn't tell him,' he said, 'though I told my mam I would. I thought he might not bring me if I told him.'

'That,' said Jan, 'was foolish in the extreme.'

She looked up to see Chris looking at her. 'Sorry if you think I was doing your job,' she said.

He shook his head. 'I might have spotted it in time,' he said. 'But you did it first. Good on you.'

After that things were straightforward. They decided that all three should go to hospital, as it was best to have a check-up. They phoned ahead, and arranged to have an ambulance waiting. The police were informed—they were very exact about all this. Everything had to be done according to the book.

'Our second rescue together,' Chris said, as they took the equipment back to the surgery.

'If we keep it as calm as this, then we'll cope,' she said.

CHAPTER THREE

CHRIS drove home to his own cottage, but didn't get out of his car. He felt restless. It was getting late but for a moment he considered driving out of the village, finding somewhere wild and lonely, and going for a walk. Anything to calm him down. But he'd been on the fells all evening, and now the weather had changed. He listened to the rain rattling on the car roof, and decided not to go. It would be foolish. He stepped out of the car and ran to his front door.

He was restless. He made himself a cup of tea, found he didn't want it. He picked up the whisky bottle, put it down again. He switched on the TV, there was nothing of even the most remote interest. He didn't bother to pick up a newspaper or a book.

Eventually he sat in an armchair, breathed deeply and tried to force himself to be calm.

While he'd been abroad he'd learned that there were times when there was nothing to do but sit and wait. Even though he knew that there were people nearby who desperately needed his care. But often circumstances meant that it was too dangerous or too difficult to move. So if there was nothing you could do, you just sat and accepted the situation.

He remembered his anger when he had gone with a disaster management team to an area that had been suffering devastating floods. It had only been about three months after he'd first arrived in Bangladesh. The three-man team had found themselves marooned on a tiny island, surrounded by flood waters. There had been a storm and a mile away there had been a village that desperately needed help. But there had been no boats.

'We have to do something,' Chris had shouted at the team leader. 'People are dying out there, we have to help them somehow. Let's just go!'

'It won't help very much if we're killed ourselves,' had been the dry retort. 'The best thing you can do to help now is to get some sleep. That way you'll be fit for tomorrow.'

It was a hard lesson, but in time he'd learned it. And slowly, the anger he'd felt had disappeared. Getting angry benefited no one.

So slowly he calmed himself.

He knew he was restless because of Jan. He thought of her, how attractive she had looked in the burgundy dress. Why was he so interested? He hadn't wanted to come back here. He'd got used to not seeing Jan, he'd been reasonably happy, he didn't want her interfering with his life again.

But now he'd met her again and he was confused. There had been two warring feelings inside him. First, she had in effect been his first true love. And he had loved her—with an intensity that had made what had followed even harder to take. And that was the second feeling—a feeling of anger and mammoth betrayal. She couldn't trust him!

The two feelings were now back. It was interesting to note that, like him, she had neither forgotten nor forgiven. She hadn't even understood why he had come back. All she knew was that he was causing her pain.

Perhaps he ought to tell his uncle he would leave. That he hadn't thought it would be as bad as it was. Then his native obstinacy took over. He would not do what she expected of him.

Finally he became more honest with himself. He wanted to stay because he was still attracted to her. But of course, it was purely physical.

After a few days Jan found she could work with Chris, largely by avoiding him. She kept out of the staff lounge when he was likely to be there. She had her own clinics, her own rounds, and she didn't need to take him with her again. If she needed to speak to a doctor, she went to John.

So she didn't see much of him. But she was always conscious that he was there. She might catch sight of him opening a door in the corridor. Then there would be a quick insincere smile and a speedy escape past him. He was there, but he didn't have to affect her. Still, it irritated her when she saw his return smile and realised that he knew exactly what she was doing.

It was a week before they had to work together again. It was her well-woman's clinic. Usually she ran it on her own, but occasionally she thought that her patients should see a doctor as well as the nurse. This week she had a patient who she thought needed to see a doctor—and John had allocated Chris to work with her. He would work in her room, see her notes. Well, so be it. They could be professional together.

When he came to her room she handed him the notes. 'Mrs Sledmere.'

Chris read through the notes, frowned and said, 'There's nothing apparently wrong. You examined her last week, her results are here, they're fine. She appears to be a reasonably normal fifty-year-old. What's the problem?'

'I don't know,' Jan said. 'I can't work it out. She's got a persistent cough and headache that comes and goes. It goes when we treat it but it still worries me. Occasionally she has a raised temperature. But not too much. Oh, and she's losing weight, very slightly. I'm convinced that there's something wrong somewhere.'

'Woman's intuition?'

'Nurse's intuition. A man once told me that medicine is an art as much as a science.'

'Some men should know when to keep their mouths shut,' he said. 'Let's have her in.'

He was good with Mrs Sledmere. He gave her a thorough examination—paying particular attention to listening to her chest. He also seemed interested in her neck. After the examination they had a long talk, largely about her recent holiday in Asia. Jan was impressed by the way he managed to ease facts out of her that had previously been hidden. They talked about her life, her work, her family, her hobbies.

'I think,' he said finally, 'that I'd like you to have a couple more tests, Mrs Sledmere. For a start, I want you to have a chest X-ray.'

'But I had one only last year! And I was fine.'

'I'm sure you were. But I'd just like another one. And I'd like a sputum sample as well.'

'But what's wrong with me?'

'Possibly nothing. We're just testing, Mrs Sledmere. We'll

know more when we have the results of the tests. Now, let's get you an appointment for the X-ray.'

'Well,' Jan said after Mrs Sledmere had left. 'What did I miss?'

'I don't know that you missed anything. But it's something that I've had quite a lot of experience of abroad. I could hear a crackle in her chest. Nodes in her neck were slightly enlarged. Weight loss, mild fever, recent visit to Asia. I suspect that Mrs Sledmere has tuberculosis.'

'Tuberculosis!'

'It's getting common in Britain again because of travel and immigration.'

'I should have spotted it.'

'You would have in time,' Chris said laconically. 'But you did something just as good. You spotted that something was seriously wrong even when the patient didn't.'

'Perhaps,' said Jan. Then she thought. 'Tuberculosis is a notifiable disease, isn't it? Mrs Sledmere isn't going to like that.'

'It's notifiable, but it's in the early stage yet. If it is tuberculosis. We can cure her quite easily.'

'Well, you can tell her if the results are positive. You detected it.' Jan checked her watch. 'The next patient isn't here for fifteen minutes,' she said. 'I usually have a break, a cup of tea about now. So if you want to go and get one...'

'Are you coming?'

'No. I need to catch up on these notes.'

'Carry on, then.' And he left. She didn't know why but Jan felt just a little sorry that he had gone so quickly.

But two minutes later the door was kicked open and there was Chris—carrying two mugs of tea.

'Oh! I didn't mean you to... And I do have to see to these notes.'

'You carry on, I won't disturb you. I'll just sit here quietly and read.'

So she tried but she just couldn't do it. He did sit there quietly and read, but he also disturbed her. She was constantly aware of his still body, of the pure white shirt with the arm muscles showing through, of the thoughtfulness in his eyes when he glanced at her. She just couldn't work! His presence filled the room.

She was glad when the phone rang. Anything to keep her mind off...things. It was her garage.

'Andy Dixon here, Jan. Been having a look at your Land Rover. It's getting on a bit, isn't it? And it hasn't exactly had what you might call regular servicing.'

'Sorry, Andy,' she muttered. 'So how much will it cost to fix it?'

She heard him grunt. 'It's not so much the parts, it's the labour. First, you need a full service. Then the steering is fine, but the brakes really need attention, front and back. You need discs replaced on the front brakes, shoes on the back and the hydraulics bled.'

'How much are we talking, Andy?'

She blanched at his answer. '*How* much? OK, I'll get back to you.' She rocked back in her chair, shaken. She could afford it, of course—but it would make a big hole in her budget. And so soon after her holiday!

'Bad news?' Chris asked, and she was still so shocked that, although it was none of his business, she told him what Andy had said.

'Full service and brakes,' Chris said, 'and there'll be the

other things he comes across. About eight hours' work.' She saw him frown. 'Would you like me to do it for you next Saturday?'

'What?' Jan couldn't believe what she had just heard.

'I'm offering to fix your Land Rover,' he said. 'You get me the parts I specify and I'll fix it next Saturday.'

'You? What do you know about car mechanics?'

'In fact, quite a lot,' he said. 'And especially a lot about Land Rovers. I told you that when the fuse went on your fuel pump. Often those I drove abroad were ancient rickety things, and if they did break down, it was always miles to the nearest mechanic. So I learned to do the job myself. It was often the only way I could get to see my patients, stop people dying.'

Now Jan was getting used to the idea and it seemed more incredible than ever. 'Why should you want to spend time working on my car? We're not friends, we don't even like each other.'

He shrugged. 'I like mechanical things, working on engines. I can lose myself in the work. And engines aren't like people, they're not awkward or lying or confused. I get a sense of completion when I've worked on a car. And, besides, the practice needs you to have a good car.'

There was a moment's pause, and he stared past her at the charts on her wall. 'You say we don't like each other. Perhaps that's true. But we used to like each other...a lot.'

'That was then,' she said. 'Things have changed and...'

'Things have changed,' he agreed. 'Now, for I don't know what reason, I've offered to fix your car. Shall I phone the garage and get them to order what will be needed?'

She looked at his face, trying to read what message was there. It was impossible; she had no idea what he was thinking. There was just a pleasant bland expression. This was a new Chris. She always used to be able to guess his thoughts—sometimes even before he did. 'I still don't know why you want to do this. Why do something for me?'

'I told you, I'm doing it entirely for myself. Now, shall I phone the garage?'

A bit of her thought that this was perhaps not a good idea. It brought them together, something she was trying to avoid. But...it would save her money. 'All right,' she said, 'phone the garage.' And then, hesitantly, 'Thanks.'

'No problem.' He looked at his watch. 'I think we're about ready to see our next patient. What's Mavis Chalmers's problem?'

'She claims it's irritable bowel syndrome. But Mavis's biggest problem is that she can't stop talking.'

He came to see her a bit later on. 'I've phoned the garage, talked to your pal Andy Dixon, we've sorted out what I'll need and he'll put it in the car when you collect it. He says you're all right to drive it for a couple of days—but take it very carefully. I've got tools of my own, but Andy is going to lend me a couple of ramps. I saw there was a flat concrete drive in front of your house, I can work there. Say if I arrive about eleven on Saturday morning?' The tone of his voice was level, almost detached.

'Great,' she said. 'Chris, I don't know what to say. I'm very grateful.'

'I'm doing it because I want to work on something mechanical again.'

She looked at him, had that sudden shock as she became aware of his body again. It happened from time to time. She didn't know why, she was quite used to seeing him now, but occasionally his very masculinity seemed to overwhelm her. He was dressed in a white coat, every inch the doctor. But his face...

'How are you going to get back home this evening?' he asked, 'if your car is at the garage?'

'I've arranged a lift with Martha, our receptionist,' she said. 'We enjoy having a little chat.' She suspected he had been about to ask her if she wanted a lift. And she didn't.

Things were moving too fast for her. She had half a mind to tell him she didn't want him to work on her car; it would be simpler for all concerned if it was mended at the garage. But now it was too late. He had ordered the stuff he would need. Jan was confused. What was happening?

Things were made worse for her that afternoon. She had practically finished her day's work, was just tidying her desk before going home, when the phone rang. The voice on the line was crisp, decisive. 'Jan? Penny Driscoll here. Glad I caught you before you went home.'

Jan smiled. 'Penny? Good to hear from you. I've been meaning to ring, apart from anything else, about Mrs Thwaite up at High Force Farm. You left me a message about her.'

'Doris Thwaite. I knew her years ago as Doris Badham. And there were two or three cases of Graves's Disease among the Badhams. Not local people, they came from near Lancaster.'

'That bit of information was useful. We've started her treatment now.'

'Good. Jan, why didn't you tell me that Chris Garrett was back?' Typical of Penny. Cut straight to what she wanted to know.

'Well he's only here for a couple of months,' Jan hedged. 'I didn't think you'd be interested.'

'Of course I'm interested. I liked the lad, thought he had a lot of good medicine in him. And I was sorry when the pair of you split up. How are you coping with having him on the doorstep again?'

'We're managing. We work together, we're polite to each other.'

'I see.'

Jan suspected that Penny saw a lot more than she had intended to divulge. The older woman went on, 'Well, if you're working together, you can bring him round to see me.'

'I'm not sure that'd be a good idea, Penny. I'll come on my own.'

Penny snorted. 'Remember, you're the community nurse and he's a doctor, for a while one of the Garrett practice. I'm just a poor retired old woman and I'm actually your patient. Perhaps I feel ill. So I want to see you both.'

'You're the poor old retired woman who works a garden the size of a small farm. You keep bees, ducks and chickens. You won half the prizes at the last horticultural show. All the years I've known you, you've never had a day's illness, and you're not going to start now.'

'How about some time this evening? I'll give you a jar of home-made honey each.'

Jan knew that Penny wouldn't give up. 'I'll go along and ask him and then ring you back,' she said.

'Why exactly does Penny want to see me?'

'I thought you wanted to see her?'

'I did. I do. It's just that recently other things have been occupying my mind.'

'I've never been called an *other thing* before,' she said. 'And I've no idea why Penny wants to see us both. She doesn't usually do things without a reason.'

They were driving the ten miles to Penny's cottage. He had been delighted when he heard of the invitation, had wanted to stop and buy her some flowers.

'Penny would only scoff, and you couldn't buy flowers to match the ones in her garden. She gardens with the same dedication she used to give to her work. If you want to give her a small treat, take her some chocolate.'

'Easily done.' So now he held the largest box of chocolates that was available in Calbeck, carefully giftwrapped.

Jan felt slightly uneasy. Possibly this was nothing more than a simple social call. Penny had been fond of Chris, perhaps she just wanted to see him again. But Jan had never told Penny exactly why the two of them had parted. She remembered what the older nurse had said. 'I won't pry. I know there's something wrong between you and if you want to tell me about it, I'll try and help. But otherwise it's your story.' And neither of them had ever referred to it again.

They parked outside Penny's cottage. It was one of a neat row of the usual grey stone cottages, the front garden a riot of colour. Jan knew that behind the cottage there was a second garden and not a weed to be seen in it anywhere.

'I'm not really sure why she wants to see us both—but if she asks, we're friends, and any trouble we might have had in the past is cleared up. OK?'

'That's more or less the truth,' he said. 'Sadly.'

Jan said nothing but went to knock on the door.

Penny looked the same as she had always done. The once grey hair was now white, but her back was as straight as it had always been. She kissed Jan and then she kissed Chris. 'Two of my favourite people,' she said briskly. 'At least,

Chris, you would have been a favourite if I'd seen more of you in the past six years. Now, come through to my back patio. I've made some tea for us.'

They sat under trellis arches overgrown with sweet-smelling climbing roses. Penny gave them tea and small sandwiches made from her home-baked bread. Jan had eaten here before with Penny, and had had some of the most delicious meals she had ever tasted.

For a while she talked to Jan about her work—asking after old patients, wanting to know what the farm gossip was. Then she questioned Chris about his work abroad, what his future plans were.

'Going to be a GP in Lincolnshire or somewhere like that? Hmm!' Obviously Penny didn't think much of the idea.

'How are you enjoying retirement, Penny?' Chris asked.

'I'm enjoying it. I'm working harder than ever but I'm not being paid as much. One day a week I give lessons in the local college, you know—I like it there. In fact, I was there last night. They have a good dramatic society, they put on a brilliant performance of *Romeo and Juliet*.'

'So you enjoyed it?' Jan asked. 'You didn't fancy yourself as the nurse in it?'

'Hmph! Certainly not. In fact, I think it's Shakespeare's most unsatisfactory play. Two star-crossed lovers indeed! Two half-baked teenagers who needed their heads knocked together.'

'So it's not like real life?'

'Unfortunately, it's too much like real life. People know what they want—but they won't go get it. Which brings me to you two.'

'Us two?' Jan asked. 'What about us two? We're not Romeo and Juliet.'

'You're showing as little sense as they did.'

'Penny, you're interfering!' Jan said. 'It's not like you.'

'Sometimes it's a community nurse's job to interfere, you should know that. And in the past when I haven't interfered, I've usually regretted it afterwards. I take it that you two hate each other as much as you did when you parted six years ago?'

Chris spoke. 'Something like that.'

'Right. By now you should be older and wiser.'

Penny put a pen and a sheet of paper in front of each of them. 'You've got ten minutes each,' she said. 'Just write down why you hate each other.'

Jan picked up the pen, then threw it down. She stood. 'I'm going. I've had enough of this. Penny, you're an old friend so I can forgive you—just. But this is nothing to do with you. And no way am I going to write on this piece of paper.'

'Chris is willing to,' Penny said calmly. 'Don't you want to know what he's got to say?'

'We said everything to each other six years ago!'

'When you were cool, calm, thoughtful and not an anguished couple of teenagers? Incidentally, I don't want to see what you write. I just want you to swap pieces of paper, see what each other felt. And I want you both to be brutally honest.'

Jan felt the tears trickling down her cheeks. 'I don't want to do this! It's hurting me!'

'I'll go back to my community nursing days again. Sometimes a boil needs lancing.'

Jan looked at Chris. He appeared calm, but his face was white. 'Do you want to take part in this...this performance?'

'Not much. But I can't see it making things any worse. It could even make them better.'

'All right, then! I'll do it.' She sat down again and grabbed for the pen.

'More tea while you're both writing?' Penny murmured. 'I'll go and make another pot.' She disappeared into the house.

Jan stared at the blank piece of paper. She saw tears drop on it, blotching the thin blue lines. Then she looked up and saw Chris staring at her. His piece of paper was blank. 'You wanted to write something,' she snapped. 'Why haven't you started?'

'I'm finding it hard,' he said. 'There's so much emotion involved that I can hardly remember the facts.'

'The facts are simple. My father died and you were responsible.'

'Possibly,' he said.

Jan bent her head and started to write. But what to write? It was all so complicated. Reluctantly, she found she had to agree with Chris. The emotion got in the way of the facts. But somehow she managed to scrawl something down.

Ten minutes later Penny returned with the full pot of tea, to find both of them madly writing. She poured three more cups, sat there and said nothing. As she sipped her own tea she saw that the other two cups were being ignored.

Finally, almost simultaneously, the two finished writing. 'Drink your tea,' Penny said. 'Don't swap the papers yet. I've a couple of things I want to say.'

She closed her eyes, and just for a moment, as she looked at the lined face, Jan realised that Penny was getting older.

'Jim Fielding, your father, I'd known him since we were both teenagers,' Penny said. 'I knew your mother, too, nursed her through that long illness. We were old, old friends. So I had to go to the inquest. Chris, you had made a statement to the police and left. Jan, you barely heard what was going on, you were so upset. So I'll remind you of the facts.

'It was summer but still a wicked night. The mountain rescue team was called out. Jim was the leader. You were there, Jan, and so was Chris. He was a doctor—just—and he'd done some of the training with you. He loved the mountains. A group was marooned on top of Carran Edge. Three of them had been climbing and they'd all fallen. One of them was losing blood rapidly, it was important to get to him as quickly as possible.'

'We know all this,' Jan said. 'How could either of us forget it?'

'Let's see. The party was doing the best it could but they knew their best wasn't good enough. The main path was straightforward but would take far too long. They weren't going to get there in time. That man needed plasma desperately. So it was decided to do something that was against the rules and possibly dangerous. The party would split, and Jim and Chris—the mountain expert and the doctor—would go ahead. There was a short cut, but it was dangerous. A path led to the bottom of a cliff face. If two men could scramble up the face, they could cut half an hour off the walking time. So that's what Chris and Jim decided to do.'

Jan was intent on this story, but she managed to glance at Chris. His already pale face had gone even whiter.

'It wasn't a good plan,' Penny went on. 'Jim slipped and fell. He broke his ankle so he couldn't go on. But he told Chris that he could make it, to carry on with the plasma and to come back later to pick him up. Chris made him as comfortable as he could and—'

'You're missing something! My father hit his head, probably when he fell. That's what he died of. A fractured skull. Any kind of doctor should have been able to detect that!'

'In the dark with only a small torch? When the patient tells him that everything is fine? Perhaps. Anyway, he was still conscious when Chris left him. Chris took the plasma to the group—to find that it wasn't necessary. The mountain rescue group from the next valley had got there before them, and the man already had his plasma. In fact, he survived. Chris led your group back to your father—and discovered he was dead. His body was carried back down the mountain. The verdict at the inquest was misadventure.'

There was silence when Penny finished. Jan could see that everyone there was busy with their own thoughts.

After a while Penny said, 'Do you want to swap papers now? And then read them…calmly? And after that I've got something more to tell you.'

Jan didn't really want to hand her paper to Chris. But she'd come so far, she thought, she may as well. He seemed reluctant to hand his paper over, too. But he did. And he even tried a small joke. 'Penny, will this happen every time we come to tea?'

'I hope not,' Penny said. 'This might be your problem—but other people are affected, too.'

Jan saw that she meant it. For a moment she wondered if all these years she had been selfish—thinking only of her own misery and not that of other people. But Chris had killed her father!

She read what Chris had written, re-read it and read it yet again. Then she opened her mouth to speak, and closed it again. She had waited six years—she could wait a little longer. Finally she and Chris looked up at each other.

'You say it was my father's decision to take the short cut. But I saw the two of you arguing, you telling him that you had to get to the party quickly.'

'It was his decision, not mine, Jan. I was surprised.'

'You never said that before.'

'You never asked. You assumed. And I felt... I didn't feel like defending myself. But it was his decision.'

Jan shook her head in vexation. Her father had been the most careful of men. 'And he didn't tell you he had hurt his head?'

'He specifically said it was only his ankle.'

'You didn't think to check?'

'I should have done. I would today. But I was young and anxious about the rescue. And he was most certain that he was all right apart from the ankle. He said he was fine and insisted that I go on. Perhaps I was negligent, but...' He shrugged.

'I said you killed him. It was what I thought. You didn't check, you left him there to die—you killed him.'

'I felt as though I had, at the time. Not that there was much that I could have done with a fractured skull halfway up a mountain. But I would have liked to have stayed with him. I would have if I'd known.' He looked at her. 'Do you believe me?'

'Yes,' she said after a while. 'And afterwards...when we argued...I said I never wanted to see you again. And you left. You didn't tell me any of this.'

'Look at what I wrote. You blamed me directly for the death of your father. And I did feel guilty for leaving him, failing him, and that made me feel angry, too. But when you blamed me, it felt like a lack of faith, a lack of trust on your part. I thought you should have been able to listen to me, at least, and some part of me thought that you should have been able to forgive me. You couldn't do either. And all that I'd thought we had together—it turned to dust. All I wanted to do was leave and forget you.'

'Did you forget me?'

'No,' he said. 'Did you forget me?'

'I couldn't. Like you, I remembered what we had and I couldn't fit that in with the man I thought had killed my father.'

'And I remembered the woman who had betrayed me when I needed her.'

'She's a woman now but she was a girl then,' Penny said gently. 'Only nineteen, remember. And you weren't much older. Now, I'm afraid there's more to this story, and neither of you knows anything about it. It might help, it might not. I'm afraid it's more misery but…Jan, remember your mother dying?'

This was the last thing she had expected. 'Yes, of course. She had lung cancer and it took her two years to die. I was sixteen when she went. One of the reasons I wanted to become a nurse was that I saw how well the Macmillan nurses looked after her, and I wanted to do as well. But I was devastated, it took me years to get over it.'

'And your dad was the same…because it took her a long time to die?'

'It nearly killed Dad. He saw a strong, cheerful, energetic woman slowly change into… And she knew, and she hated it. It was the loss of dignity. And then she died.'

She knew her voice was quavering now. Well, that was how she felt. Chris put his hand over the table, covering hers, and it was comforting. But then he withdrew it.

She looked at him, surprised, 'You wanted to hold my hand,' she said, 'but then you felt you weren't certain how I would take it.'

'True. Just for a moment I flashed back and...' He took a deep breath. 'Penny, what were you going to tell us?'

Penny frowned. 'First of all, I'm going to break a confidence. Though I swore to your father that I never would. I'm only doing it now because I think he'd approve.'

Jan looked at her, amazed. 'You swore to my father? What?'

'He died as the result of an accident. But he was going to die anyhow. He had problems, and he confided in me rather than in Dr Garrett. I'd known him longer. I went with him to see an oncologist in hospital. Your father had inoperable cancer of the bowel. I had suspected it, the oncologist confirmed it. He had at most six months to live. And most of those months would have been a time of pain and indignity and watching his family—you, Jan—suffer.'

'But I never knew!'

'He didn't want you to know. He was a proud man and he loved you.'

Jan grappled to come to terms with what she had just heard. 'So...are you telling me that an accident would have been almost a relief for him?'

'Certainly, he might have thought that way. He had nothing to lose. And I suspect that he thought that, for both you and him, a quick death would be preferable to a long, slow, painful death. Perhaps some dark corner of his mind helped him to that quick death. Perhaps that was one of the reasons he told Chris to go on.'

Jan looked from Penny to Chris and back to Penny. 'I don't know what to say or think,' she said. 'Chris, hating you has been with me for the past six years. I don't hate you any more but I feel as if something has...gone from me.'

'I know what you mean,' he muttered. 'It ought to be good

but it means that I've built much of my life on something that's not there. It's hard to cope with that.'

Penny reached for the two pieces of paper, folded them and then tore them into tiny pieces. 'I think you two have visited an old lady for long enough,' she said. 'Time you went, you've got your own business now. But you will keep in touch, won't you?'

Jan stood, walked round the table to hug the old lady. 'Do you know what you've done to us—for us?'

'I hope it's been good,' said Penny.

They were silent as Chris drove her back to her cottage. He pulled up outside, turned to look at her. 'Don't invite me in,' he said. 'Neither of us is ready for it yet. Both our lives have been turned upside down. We need to think about that.'

'I know. We've got no excuse for hating each other any more. But what's left?'

'We used to love each other, but that's gone, too. We buried it under hatred. Whatever we want, it has to start again. We're two different people, even if we're people with a past. We're almost strangers.'

'Never strangers, we shared too much. But you're right. Whatever we want, it has to start again.' She didn't want to get out of the car yet, she felt that there was something she still had to say. 'Chris, it seems… I—we—had three months that were wonderful. Then six years that were…less than wonderful. I want the future to be better. Good night, Chris.'

She leaned over, quickly kissed him on the forehead. Then she was gone.

CHAPTER FOUR

THERE was a letter waiting for Chris that night when he got home. A thick letter in an expensive envelope, with the crest of an international charity on the outside. He slit it open.

It was a job offer. A job that he had wanted for the last four years of his life.

To be exact, it was an invitation to apply for a job. But it was made more than clear that the job was his if he wanted it.

For years he had fought for extra funds for his work. Not more money for himself—the salary he had earned had been sufficient for his admittedly rather simple needs. He'd wanted more money so he could do his job properly. He'd wanted to train medical auxiliaries. He'd wanted a means of travelling and bringing the simplest of medicine to the people who'd needed it. He'd wanted an efficient emergency response unit. There had always seemed to be an emergency somewhere in his territory. He had spent all of his little spare time in writing reports to the charity, making suggestions, compiling detailed plans.

And now those funds seemed to be available. A hospital and training school would be built. And the charity wanted him as the overall director.

Just two months ago he would have been delighted at the prospect. Just two hours ago he would have been delighted. Now he wasn't so sure.

He was still struggling to make sense of the revelation that he had no good reason for hating Jan any more. And she felt the same way about him. So that meant that the emotional struggles of the past couple weeks had been pointless. Now he could admit to himself that he was still greatly attracted to her. And he didn't have to deceive himself into thinking that the attraction was purely physical. Certainly there was physical desire there. But now he could want the whole Jan—the Jan he'd thought he'd had before.

But this job. Everything he had wanted for the past six years. It would be so hard to turn down.

It was a brutal choice. Jan or the job.

Jan saw little of Chris over the next two days. That was good—they needed the time apart. Her entire life picture had altered and something told her that to rush into anything new would be dangerous. But late on Friday he knocked on her door, put his head round and asked if all was OK for the next day.

'Tomorrow?' she asked, wondering what he was talking about.

'I'm to see to your car.'

She'd forgotten. But of course it would be great to see him. 'Tomorrow is fine,' she said.

'See you about eleven.' And he was gone.

She was up early on Saturday. She cleaned an already clean house—why? She wondered what she would be expected to do. Hold his tools? Feed him? Certainly he would need the usual workman's frequent cups of tea or coffee. What else might he expect? And how had their relationship changed since they had decided they could let go of the hate? She just didn't know. She was still unsure as to exactly what she did want.

She looked outside—it was cloudy, windy, but she suspected it wasn't going to rain. She couldn't expect him to work in the rain. She felt at a loss. The situation was out of her control.

Chris came on the dot of eleven, dressed in a T-shirt and overalls. She came out and offered him a drink. 'I've just had a big breakfast,' he said. 'I'll not want anything else for a couple of hours and then I'd like a coffee. Now, if you fuss round me you'll make me nervous. You go and do what you do, and if I need anything I'll call you.'

'Right,' Jan said, feeling a little displeased at being dismissed from her own front garden. 'If that's what you want.' She thought that a little conversation for a couple of minutes might have been rather pleasant. He, apparently, did not.

She went inside. She might not be able to see him, but she was ever conscious of his presence. There was the tinkle of tools, the scrape of the ramps being placed in position, the roar of the engine as the car drove gently up them.

For ten minutes she occupied herself in some pointless household chores. Then she couldn't help herself: she peered through the window. Chris seemed utterly absorbed in what he was doing. She studied his face, it fascinated her, the way that he... What was she doing? She didn't know this man! He wasn't the Chris she had loved six years ago. Now he was an enigma.

Deliberately she went into the back garden to work, away

from the sight and sound of him. But she knew he was there. And she couldn't concentrate.

It got worse. She took him his mug of coffee at one o'clock and had her own mug ready just inside the door, in case he wanted to stop work for ten minutes and chat. He didn't want to. He gave her a brief smile of thanks, put the coffee to one side and wriggled back under the car.

Jan bent over to peer at him. 'For lunch, do you want sandwiches or something cooked, like—'

'I don't do lunch. But another coffee in a couple of hours would be great.'

'How's it going?' she asked, still desperately hoping for some kind of conversation.

'Fine. I'm enjoying myself.' Then there was the sound of metal hammering on metal.

No way could she talk over that. 'Good,' she muttered to herself, and retreated indoors.

She took him more coffee at three o'clock (but with three chocolate biscuits and a napkin to hold them with, if his hands were oily) and got a similar reception. Chris was engrossed with her car. He did not want to be engrossed with her. Well, not now anyway. Once again she remembered his capacity for absolute single-mindedness, and sighed.

'The door's open and you know where the kitchen and the bathroom are,' she said. 'Make yourself at home. I'm going to the village to get a few things.'

'Fine. No need to hurry back.'

So that was that. Dismissed from her own front garden again. In something of a temper, Jan walked to the village to do her weekend shopping.

She only intended to be an hour, and when she got back,

she promised herself, Chris was going to be fed a sandwich whether he wanted one or not. And they were going to chat for a while, like civilised human beings. But it didn't happen.

She was the community nurse; everyone in the village knew her. So when a little girl fell over in the high street and gashed her knee rather badly, it was Jan who took the little girl home, dressed the knee, reassured the worried mother that all would be well. And then she just had to accept a cup of tea. So when she got back to her own cottage, Chris had gone.

He wasn't fixing her car. He had already finished; the car was down from the ramps; and there was a note pinned to her door. *Job done, all seems well. Happy motoring!*

She felt disappointed. It would have been polite to be able to say thank you.

She couldn't just wait till Monday to thank him. He'd spent the greater part of the day working on her car.

She decided she'd been casual enough recently so, instead of the jeans and shirt she'd had on, she put on a pretty striped yellow dress. Anyway, the wind had dropped and there was a pleasant evening sun. She took one of the bottles of wine she'd brought back from her holiday and drove round to his cottage. Just a small thank-you, she told herself. I'd do it for anyone.

No one answered when she rang his doorbell. But his car was outside so he must be in. She rang again. And a moment later the door was opened—by a wet man dressed solely in a towel.

She blinked. 'You're having a bath.' Only after a moment did she realise that it hadn't been the brightest thing to say.

He didn't seem to mind. 'Just had one,' he corrected. 'Come in. Or does it seem proper to be invited into a house by a naked man? We might be seen.'

'I'll take the risk. After all, I am the community nurse. People will think that I've told you to take your trousers off so I can give you an injection.'

'The very thought upsets me. Now, sit down a moment while I go and get dressed.'

She wasn't sure how it had happened but somehow she had come through the door and into his living room. She lifted the bottle she had brought, now encased in a cheerful bottle bag. 'But I only came here to give you this and—'

'I won't be a minute. I was already out of the bath.' He disappeared upstairs so she had to sit down.

She looked around. She'd never been in this cottage before, though she knew it was rented, usually on long lets. The furniture appeared quite pleasant, the decor would do. But apart from a set of medical texts on a bookshelf, and a computer in a corner, there was no sign of Chris trying to make his mark on the place. It was as impersonal as a hotel room.

A couple minutes later he came down the stairs, now dressed in light chinos and shirt, his hair tousled. He looked…he looked… She refused to admit the word she had thought of. She still didn't know what she thought of this new Chris.

'I saw you'd finished the car, and I wanted to thank you,' she said. 'I would have been back before but I had to perform a bit of light first aid in the village. Anyway, I brought you this bottle.'

'There's no need for thanks, I enjoyed myself.'

There was a minute's silence. He just looked at her and she felt uncomfortable. 'How do you like living in this cottage?' she asked after a while, slightly aggressively. 'You don't appear to have made much of a home of it. There's no personal touches.'

He shrugged. 'The cottage is fine. Over the past few years I've got used to living out of a big travelling bag. I've never been in one place for too long, and I seem to have lost the home-building urge. If there's hot water and a clean, dry bed, then that's enough for me.'

'Seems a bit spartan to me. Now...Chris, you've done a great job on my car, and you've saved me a lot of money so at least I'd like to—'

His voice was quiet. 'Jan? You're surely not going to offer to pay me? That would be unforgivable.'

Yes, it would. She blushed at the very thought. 'No! I... It's just that... Well, in some way I'd like to say thank you. You've helped me, but we still don't quite know what we feel about each other, and...' She was conscious that she was making a mess of this and she didn't like it. Usually she coped quite well with difficult social situations, but this seemed a harder one than usual.

'There is one thing,' he said. 'I've not stopped so far today—largely because I've been enjoying myself. But now I'm quite hungry. I was going to boil myself a couple of eggs, but if you wanted to cook a meal for me, that would be great.'

He lifted the bag she had put on the table and peered inside. 'That's not a wine I recognise but I'm sure it'll be great. Could you cook something to go with it?'

The question bewildered her. 'We could go round to the Bull,' she said. 'I'll buy you dinner. They do—'

'The Bull will be very busy. We'd have to wait, we might not even get a seat. And I'd rather you cooked for me.' Then he paused a moment, before adding quietly, 'If you dare.'

That was a challenge she couldn't avoid. 'I certainly dare,' she said, and stood. 'The question is, why do you want me to cook?'

He grinned. 'I want to see if you've progressed. To see if you're still the girl who made sandwiches for our picnic. Corned beef, grated cheese, pickle, lettuce and mayonnaise. That was one sandwich! And all between two thick slices of wholemeal bread. I could barely fit it into my mouth.'

'You managed somehow, as I remember. And came back for more.'

'True. Happy memories.'

They were happy memories—now—and the thought of them brought back a combined joy and pain that was almost unendurable.

'I think my catering has improved a little since then. Give me an hour and come round. I need time to get things ready.'

'An hour,' he agreed. 'I'll be there.'

Her heart was beating hard as she left his cottage. She had not expected this. She didn't know if she wanted this. She didn't hate Chris any more—but she wasn't sure what was going to fill the vacuum. Then, to her amazement, she felt another, totally alien emotion. She was looking forward to cooking for him, just being with him. This was madness!

She knew that she could do something simple—tinned soup and beans on toast sort of thing. But she felt a sense of pride, of determination. She knew, or remembered, what he liked to eat. He had always loved curries—but mild ones. 'I like to taste the spices,' he had once told her. 'With too many vindaloos, getting through them is a test of your manhood rather than a pleasant gastronomic experience.'

She liked cooking curries—so she would do him one, and a salad side dish. As she turned into her drive, she was already thinking of what she had in stock. The first thing to do would be to change. This was not a dress for cooking in.

Concentrating on cooking stopped her thinking about why she was going to so much trouble. For a while she lost herself in her work. When the curry was gently bubbling, the rice steaming and the salad dressed, there was the table to set. And finally she went upstairs, had another quick shower, changed back into her yellow dress and quickly rearranged her hair.

Then downstairs, to sit and compose herself. He'd arrive in five minutes' time, she knew he'd be punctual. Time to calm herself. But sitting and thinking wasn't calming.

It was exciting.

When Chris arrived she saw that he had also changed. He was wearing smart black trousers and a formal light blue shirt that looked as if it was made of silk. She had to admit to herself, he looked good.

He handed her her bottle back and a bag with another bottle in it. Also, a small parcel wrapped in gold paper. 'Not much scope in the village shop,' he said, 'I was going to bring flowers but they had none. But I got another bottle of wine, and this is just for you.'

She pulled away the gold paper. Inside was a bar of plain dark chocolate: exactly what she loved. She disliked fancy chocolates that were too sweet and had little taste. 'You remembered what I like,' she said.

'I remembered.'

She liked that.

She invited him to sit on her couch for a drink before dinner. And when they both had a glass in their hands, she leaned forward and said curiously, 'Why are we doing this? I know we don't hate each other any more. But we don't know what emotion to put in place of the hatred.'

'That's true,' he said.

'So why are you forcing me? You mend my car, you want a meal with me…and every time I meet you I get the same feeling, a sort of wondering. I feel sad that I've missed something over the past six years. I see…I see…'

'What do you see?'

'It doesn't matter,' she said. 'Just tell me why you came back here to Calbeck.'

He shrugged. 'You know as well as I do. To put it crudely, you're unfinished business… I think you feel the same. Perhaps it's something we both need to come to terms with. The easiest thing is to see each other and see what happens.'

'Are you frightened?'

'No,' he said. 'I'm angry and I'm determined. And every time I look at you I feel something I daren't put a name to.'

'You daren't?' Her voice was hoarse.

'I daren't. Not yet. But soon I will.'

There didn't seem to be anything to add to that. And so she said, 'Well, on that note, shall we have dinner now?'

She led him to the alcove she used as her dining room, indicating where he was to sit. The time for emotion seemed to be over, now it was just getting to know each other.

'You've gone to a lot of trouble in the past hour,' he said as he picked up his napkin. 'This all looks marvellous. And your house, too, you seem really comfortable in here. This is a home. Different from where I live.'

She was pleased at his compliment. 'I sold my father's house,' she told him. 'It was too big, and I just couldn't face living there. I bought this place and spent an awful lot of money having it renovated. And now I love it here.'

For the first course she had made a simple salad, with cheese from a local farm. She indicated he was to start. He tasted the salad, then commented, 'You're a home-maker. Why aren't you married, Jan? You could make some man very happy.'

She wondered if he was being ironic. But she said sharply, 'It's not my aim in life to make a man happy. In fact, I got very close to being married.'

'So someone told me. You were nearly married to a Peter Harris—the exact words were that you were sort of engaged.' He looked at her curiously. 'Sort of engaged? You were never a "sort of" person—everything you did was wholehearted. What kind of dedication is that? What happened? Do you mind telling me?'

She would tell him, but probably not the full truth. 'We loved each other,' she said. 'But we had different interests, different ideas about the life we each wanted to live. I wanted children, he said definitely he did not. So in the end, very sadly, we decided to part. And it hurt.'

She didn't tell him that it had never been a very passionate love affair. And that when it had ended, both had felt a certain sense of relief. But she saw how Chris's eyes flicked towards her, and wondered if he suspected the truth. She felt angry, as if she had let her guard down.

She hurried to the kitchen, fetching small dishes of sambals, poppadoms, a steaming tureen of Basmati rice and two dishes of curry—one lamb, one vegetable. He looked at the feast incredulously.

'You've cooked this in the last hour?'

'I love curry,' she said, 'I cook it often. There's nothing special about this.'

In fact, there was something special, but she was not going to tell him that. And she had been to a curry-cooking course, run by the chef from a local Indian restaurant, and had learned a lot from him. She knew her curries were good.

They ate for a while and then he said, 'This is really fantastic, Jan. I've never had a meal like it in England.'

'I would have thought that you'd eaten a lot of curries in Bangladesh.'

He shrugged. 'I've had good ones occasionally—mostly in the big cities. Out in the villages where I spent most of my time, cooking is not one of the great arts. There's often not enough food, for a start.'

'I see.' She decided to move on. 'You asked me why I wasn't married and I told you. Now you tell me why you aren't married.'

He thought for a while. 'It just never happened,' he said.

'You never fell in love?'

He thought again. 'I had quite a long affair with a nurse—when we managed to meet. We never thought about the future. Both of us guessed there wouldn't be one for us. We both were busy working, often apart for long periods, trying to cope with inadequate materials and staff, and obstructive officials. For us, what we had was just comfort—sex and pleasure. We liked each other. When we parted it was quite amicable and I still get a letter from her about every six months. But it was never like...' His voice trailed away.

She seized on this. 'Never like what?'

'Never like I thought it could be.' He paused a moment, then said, rather harshly, 'Never like it had been with you. I wanted something more like that.'

'Perhaps you have that only when you are very young. So

tell me about your work.' She still felt afraid of talking too intimately about their feelings.

This was not the way he had expected their meeting to go. She had been thinking about him—it was obvious from her questions. But not their past. She was thinking about who or how he was now.

It struck him that he had to be completely honest with her. There had been too much misunderstanding between them.

'Jan, there's something I'd better tell you. I've just had an offer of a job back in Bangladesh. Setting up and running a new hospital. I wasn't going to go back, but this is the job I've been angling for for a long time. I could do so much good there and I'm tempted.'

She concealed her feelings well. But he saw her body tense, and the polite smile she gave him was obviously insincere.

'Are you the only person who could do the job? Don't you think that perhaps you've done enough there? Do you want to go back?'

Again he had to be honest with her. 'There are others who could do the job, probably as well as I could. As to wanting to go back—I'm not sure.'

'There's nothing that makes you want to stay in England? Perhaps the GP's job in Lincolnshire that you were looking for?'

He knew that she wasn't talking about him staying in England for a job. She was asking if he wanted to stay for her. And no matter what it cost, he had to give her an honest answer. If he could.

'I'd really like to stay in England,' he said. 'Now, more than ever. But this job offer is something I must think about.'

'Of course,' she said. 'Just so long as you don't make up your mind too quickly.'

Was there just a touch of relief in her voice?

Two hours later they had finished the meal and stacked the dishes in her washer together. They had sat on her couch and finished the bottle of wine, eaten a fair amount of chocolate and talked amiably. She was surprised how at ease she felt.

They talked about his work and then hers—how things had moved on in the valley since he'd left. They talked about changes in medicine. By mutual consent they didn't talk about their past together. This was a time for the present, not the past. And the evening sped by.

Finally, and not too late, he stood. 'I'd better go,' he said. 'We must both be tired.' After a pause he went on, 'I really enjoyed myself.'

There was another pause, then she said, 'So did I.' And she had. Perhaps a little to her surprise.

She led him to the door and in the narrow hall reached past him to open it—and their bodies touched. She hadn't turned on the hall light, so they were in semi-darkness, and when she looked up at him she couldn't make out his expression, could see only the glitter of his eyes.

Perhaps for a moment they stood there. Then, very gently, his arms wrapped round her shoulders, eased her towards him. She knew she could break away. She knew that if she moved he would instantly release her, Nothing would be said, they could carry on as before. But she didn't move. Some urge that she didn't fully understand told her to stay where she was. Close to him. She knew she shouldn't be doing this, it was madness. And at the same time she knew she was not going to move.

His hands slipped further down her body, now were linked round her waist. She felt him pulling her closer to him, and happily leaned forward into the warmth of his body. They were touching properly now. She could feel her thighs against his thighs, her breasts pressed against his chest and his breath caressing her hair. She rested her cheek on his shoulder. It felt so comfortable. It felt like coming home.

She had no idea how long they stayed like that. But after a while she realised that she had to make a decision. He had come so far, done so much. Now it was up to her. She reached her arms round his waist, hugged him tight to her. And she lifted her head.

His body was tense under her hands and she could hear his heavy breathing. It was strange: she knew exactly what he was feeling because it was what she was feeling. There was surprise, and at the same time a sense of inevitability. And also a vastly growing need.

He pulled her closer, bent and kissed her. Kissed her softly, gently, the touch like a feather, grazing her lips. It was wonderful, she thought they could stay like that for ever. But it was also a promise, of what might be, of what was to come.

And slowly the tension between them mounted. She could feel the thrumming of the blood in her veins, feel his heartbeat against her, so strong she thought she might almost hear it.

They stayed together for—seconds, minutes, hours? And Jan found a growing insistence inside her. She couldn't bear it. She just could not go on like this for ever. Wildly, she wondered if this was a competition. Were they to stay like this until one of them broke, one of them gave way to the feelings that were tearing through both of their bodies?

She could stand it no longer. She heard the half-fearful sob that she gave, and then she wrapped her hand round his neck, forced him to her in a kiss that was as passionate as the previous one had been restrained.

He held her head. His tongue found her open lips, slid inside her mouth in a symbolic act that brought a terrifying pleasure and the promise of more to come.

She tore at the back of his shirt, pulled it so her fingers could feel the warmth of his skin, feel the muscles that she remembered so well. And his hand did the same, flicked open the catch of her bra and then slid round to hold and caress the fullness of her breasts. She felt them grow taut, erect, and moaned with the pleasure.

Nothing happened to stop them. But suddenly a cold sneering voice inside her head said, *This man's going to leave you. Again. What do you think you're doing?*

It was a good question. And as she heard it her body tensed, and she moved away from him. He must have felt her reaction, because his arms moved from holding her tight to resting gently on her waist, and then fell away altogether. The only sound was that of their breathing.

Somehow she managed to speak without a quaver in her voice. 'This was not a good idea Chris,' she said. 'I think you'd better go now.'

'Why wasn't it a good idea?' His voice was ragged. 'It was something we both wanted—both needed.'

'Too much too soon,' she said. 'And I do want and need you. But now I've learned to be cautious. I can't help it.'

'We have time,' he said. 'Jan, I'm sorry if I upset you.'

'Two of us to blame.'

He reached for the door, opened it. Then he turned and said, 'I half lied then. I'm certainly not in the least sorry that

I kissed you.' Before she knew what he was doing he had bent forward, snatched another kiss. 'Goodnight, Jan,' he said. And he was gone.

No matter how hard the day, Jan always cleaned up at night before going to bed. There wasn't much mess now, but she shook off the tablecloth, took bottles and glasses into the kitchen, straightened cushions. Then she made herself a going-to-bed cup of cocoa. There was one square of chocolate left, so she ate it. And she sat on the couch to think.

What had happened? What had she done?

She didn't know what she felt about Chris. She could see his good points now, and what had been there before had been erased from her mind. Certainly she had loved him once—or had thought she had. But that had been six years ago: she was a different person now. She had managed without him—even been happy without him. She had contemplated marrying someone else.

But never had she felt anything like the physical joy he had brought her. And for a moment that joy had returned. She had remembered the joy, remembered what she had missed for so long.

But he had been honest with her. The harsh fact was that there was something that he thought might be more important than her. This job. He had told her that he might be leaving, and she couldn't cope with more heartache. So what to do?

The best thing was to forget what had happened. It was her body remembering, not her brain. And as he had said, they had time. She would cope. She always had done in the past.

She went to bed. When she was half-asleep, in that happy

state when consciousness can be manipulated, she thought of Chris. She thought of being kissed by him. And how wonderful it would be if he were there every night to kiss her.

CHAPTER FIVE

WHEN Jan went to work on Monday morning she wondered how things would be between them. She was half-afraid that Chris would come to see her, would ask for some kind of assurance or statement. She knew they both would want this in time. But not quite yet.

And she didn't think about the kiss, about how she had felt. Part of her even hoped that the memory would dim a little, then she wouldn't have to consider what she had done—no, what they had done. And how magical it had been.

She would love it if he came and said that he'd thought about the job abroad and was going to turn it down.

In the meantime, she lost herself in her work. There was always plenty of that.

She received a phone call, semi-official, from one of her friends in Social Services. After a bit of prompting, someone at his school had questioned Ben Mackie's son about the bruises on his face. As a result Social Services had made a home visit, and Ben had been less than co-operative—at first.

'So we sent in one of our newer members of staff to talk to him,' her friend said cheerfully. 'He's an ex-policeman, six foot four inches tall, very earnest, very anxious to make sure that his clients know what is expected of them and what the penalties might be if Ben didn't behave. Doubt we'll have any more bruising.'

'Good,' said Jan. She liked it when different authorities could work together.

In the middle of the morning, John called her in.

'How are Mr and Mrs Thwaite up at High Force Farm?' he asked.

Jan looked at him thoughtfully. 'Well, Doris is fine. Or getting better would be more accurate. Since Chris diagnosed the hyperthyroidism she's been on antithyroid drugs and she's got a new lease of life.'

'And Herbert?'

Jan sighed. 'There's no talking to him. He won't take drugs, he won't behave. I just don't know what to say about him. It'd kill him and it'd kill Doris if he had to go into some kind of sheltered accommodation. But they can't carry on as things are.'

'You're right. In fact, Doris has just phoned. She's asked if Chris can go out with you—apparently Herbert quite took to him. Might pay some attention to him.'

'Instead of to a mere woman like me,' Jan said cheerfully. 'Well, I've seen it all before. Is Chris free this afternoon?'

'He will be,' John said. 'Incidentally, how are you getting on with him?'

Jan looked at him, knowing that there was a lot left unasked in that question. 'He's a good doctor. We're getting on fine. I...like him.'

'That's good to hear. He's my only living relative, and I'm fond of him. And nothing would give me greater pleasure than to see him take over here when I retire. But...you can't order people's lives to suit yourself. So, the Thwaite family this afternoon.'

'Looking forward to it.'

They made an early start. It was a glorious day, the sun shining, the air like champagne. It made her feel glad to be alive, certain that whatever problems she might have, they could be solved. And she had to admit, it felt good to have Chris sitting by her side.

'I phoned you yesterday,' he said as soon as they were on their way. 'Two or three times. But there was no answer.'

'I went over to the coast. There's a girl I trained with who lives there and she's about to get married. So we had a hen afternoon.'

'Did you discuss marriage?' She knew he was making gentle fun of her.

'We did indeed. And we came to the same conclusion. If you get the right man, then marriage can be heaven. I didn't emphasise the word "if" too much.'

'Always the tactful one. When's the ceremony?'

'In a couple of weeks. The invitation is for me and a partner, if I have one.'

'I see. And do you have a partner?'

'I'm running down the possibles and trying to choose,' she said. 'Don't worry, you're somewhere on the list.'

'That makes me feel good. Anyway, I've not had the chance to say how much I enjoyed your curry.'

'Thank you,' she said. And she decided that if things were to be said, she'd start by saying them herself. 'I wasn't myself, you know. Perhaps I was tired after the week. I had a bit too much to drink and so I acted…foolishly. I hope you'll see that was the case and just forget things.'

'Things? You mean that I kissed you?'

She forced herself to remain calm. 'That's what I mean. I didn't quite know what I was doing.'

She felt a bit ashamed of herself for offering this excuse—because she knew it was just an excuse, and suspected that he knew that too.

'Well, I knew what I was doing. And it was marvellous.'

'Chris! I'm still trying to make sense of things. And you saying you were thinking of going back to Bangladesh—that threw me a little. In fact, it threw me a lot. As for you kissing me—it started all sorts of ideas, memories, worries. I'm trying to cope and I still don't know how to feel.'

'But it was marvellous, wasn't it?'

'Yes,' she sighed. 'It was marvellous.' After a moment she found that the confession had made her feel rather better so she added to it. 'I guess it was the real me that kissed you, Chris. And the real me wanted to carry on kissing you.'

There was silence for a while.

'That is a lovely thing to hear.'

For a while there was silence between them. She thought about what she had just said. She felt liberated. Now she had confessed that she had liked it, perhaps he would kiss her again. She hoped so.

Presently he said, 'We're going up to High Force Farm. Are you going to take the main road?'

'I usually do. It's longer but it's faster.'

'There's another route, along the Sharonbrook Valley. Could we go that way? It's a fine day, we could enjoy the view.'

She tensed. 'Why should you want to drive along the Sharonbrook Valley?'

'Neither of us has much to do. And we're early for our appointment.'

'No other reason?'

'Is there a reason why you don't want to go that way?'

'Chris, you're playing with me. And I half like it, half don't.' But five minutes later she wrenched at the wheel and swerved off to the right along the Sharonbrook Valley. The road here was beautiful, narrow, following the course of the river. And it was lonely.

She said nothing, her hands clenched tight on the wheel, her eyes screwed up. She was unaware of the beauty around her—and aware that he was unaware, too. He was looking at her but she couldn't read his expression.

The car was rocking, bouncing over the ruts, skidding on the mud at corners. She was going far too fast.

After a while he said, 'Driving like this won't make the memories go away, Jan.'

'Do I want them to go away? Why did you bring me here?'

'You made me want to come. I've not been here in six years, I wanted to see the place again. How often have you been down here, Jan?'

'Never. I always take the main road, it's faster.'

His voice was quiet. 'Is that really the reason?'

'Of course it isn't! This place brings back memories that I thought I wanted to forget. I didn't want them reawakened.'

'And now?'

'Now the memories are all happy. If anything, I'm frightened of a kind of time slip. A little bit of me is worried that suddenly I'll feel towards you the way I used to.'

'And would that be a bad thing?'

She smiled sadly. 'I'm a different person now, Chris. We both are. I'm happy with the past, but now I want a future.'

'So do I. And remember, whatever we did, we did together.'

She was still unsure, suspected that he was, too. They were so close to each other, but each was afraid of making that last, absolute commitment. She wondered how the place they were going to visit would affect them.

She glanced at the hillside above her and suddenly came to an abrupt stop. Then the engine roared as she drove off the road and set off up a rough track that seemed to be nearly vertical, so it was a good thing that the Land Rover was a four-wheel-drive.

'Why are you going so fast?' he asked.

'You wanted to wander down memory lane. Now so do I and I'm in a hurry. We can get as far as the quarry this way.'

'Not if you kill us first,' he said cheerfully.

She carried on driving as fast as she had been, just to show him that she was in charge, but then slowed to a more reasonable pace. And then they arrived.

There was a tiny quarry, nearly at the top of the hill, worked out and abandoned years ago. Jan drove into the quarry floor, braked and turned off the engine. For a moment she stared sightlessly through the windscreen, then she and Chris climbed out of the car. She locked the doors behind them.

'Shall we go?' she asked. 'Go and see and remember what we did?'

'Would you like to?'

'I don't know,' she said. 'I think I'd like to but I'm a bit afraid. It's not the memories, it's the present that's worrying me.'

'I'd like to go and just for a moment remember how we were,' he said. 'But the present is much more important. I'd like to go with you, Jan. But I want you to come peacefully and happily. What happened up here was one of the magic moments of my life. Probably *the* magic moment. I'd like to keep the magic. And I won't keep the magic if you're sad or regretful.'

For a moment she said nothing. She looked around at the blue skies, the mossy grey of the stone on the quarry walls. She heard distant birdsong, felt the warmth of the sun on her face. Then she looked at Chris. She didn't know what he was thinking; the open-faced lad she used to know had long gone. But she suspected he was sharing some of her thoughts. And a calmness came to her.

'What we hoped for then, promised each other here, has long gone away,' she said. 'Though I do remember it as magic.'

'Perhaps we can revisit, the memory, the magic,' he said. 'We've had different lives, followed different paths. But we're entitled to memories. They make life what it is. And there is still the future. This place might help us know what it is to be. There might be a greater magic in the future.'

That thought caught her by the throat. She couldn't speak.

She stood there looking at the wood, her thoughts rioting. She couldn't move. Then he put his hand to her shoulder and urged her forward. Gently she shook off his hand, started walking. She didn't want him to touch her, she needed to keep herself under control. But then she thought, Why not? And reached for his hand to hold.

They walked to the far wall of the quarry, scrambled upwards. Then they were into the wood and he led her along a faintly visible path. It was dark here, the trees meeting overhead.

Neither of them spoke. She had a head that was buzzing not with memories but with hopes for the future. Perhaps he had, too.

After ten minutes he stopped and looked around. Then he led her off the path, climbing upwards through the trees until they were on the edge of the wood, looking at a great stretch of open land. There was nothing human to be seen, only the great sweep of grass and then the jagged edge of mountains behind. They walked a while until they came to a little hollow in the grassland. A place where, if they were lying down, people couldn't be seen.

He stopped and looked at her.

'Yes, it was here,' she said. 'Though I've never been back since.'

He sat on a little stone outcrop. She moved and sat facing him, folding her arms. It struck her how silent it was. There was no sound of wind, no cry of birdsong. Only their two voices in the wilderness.

'Why did you bring me here?'

He shrugged. 'We started new lives when we were at Penny's. Now we have to make sense of the past. And, for me, this is a good place to start.' There was more silence and then he went on, 'We were young then. Not capable of knowing what life had to offer.'

To her amazement she found that she was grinning, a mischievous grin. 'You must have had some idea of what life could offer. You brought a packet of condoms with you.'

He laughed, obviously embarrassed. 'Yes, I did. Apart

from anything else—a few weeks before I'd been to a lecture from a woman professor. She told us that everyone should be accountable for their actions. And that unwanted pregnancies were a disgrace.'

'So did you intend to seduce me when we came here?'

'Seduce?' He managed a wan smile. 'A nice Victorian word. No, I had no specific intentions. And I think that whatever we did, we did together.'

'We seduced each other,' she said. 'And I remember you were so good to me, Chris. You offered to stop two—no, three times. And you meant it, too.'

'I was as scared as you were,' he said bluntly. 'Though it wasn't my first time. I just felt that with you, things had to be exactly right.'

'Nice to be young, wasn't it? It's a pity we had to grow up.'

The sun was warm on her face. She leaned back, stretched out full length on the turf. 'I want to be quiet a minute,' she said. 'I just want to think.'

'Whatever you want,' he said.

They had driven almost casually along by the Sharonbrook Valley that day years ago. But it had been too pleasant an evening to drive for long, so they had parked the car and walked up to the quarry. And then through the wood and then, by accident, up to here. Had it been an accident? For a while she had thought it had been planned by providence.

Chris had spread his nylon anorak on the ground and she had lain on it. He lay by her side. It had been warm then— as it was warm now. She had felt the sun on her face then, as she felt it now. And for a couple seconds she was transported back to that time.

He had lain by her side, his arm under her head. He had pulled him to her and kissed her. He had kissed her often enough before—they had enjoyed many ecstatic half-hours in the darkness as they'd walked to her home, or by the side of the barn at the foot of her farm.

And in time they had come to this secluded grassy hollow, and here they had made love. For her the physical side had been both awkward and wonderful. She hadn't minded it being awkward, because she had known it would get better. And he was so careful with her! What had stayed in her mind had been the love, the memory of them giving to each other.

Could they give themselves to each other again?

'Perhaps it's time we should go.'

His voice was soft, but it brought Jan crashing back to reality. She looked at her watch, realised she hadn't moved or spoken for fifteen minutes. 'Were you dozing or were you remembering?' he asked.

She was confused, didn't want to answer. 'What were you doing?' she challenged.

'I was remembering.'

'So was I. I remember thinking that things would never change. But they did.'

'Yes, they changed,' he said sadly. Then he thought. 'Could they change again?'

'Anything is possible.'

She saw him jerk violently upright, look at her with an intensity far removed from the gentleness previously on his face.

'Jan, the past is over! Good or bad, it's over! Remember the saying—today is the first day of the rest of your life? Well, it's true. We've got to live for now.'

Then he came and kissed her. A passionate, demanding

kiss that seared her senses. And finally when their kiss stopped he still looked at her, those blue eyes seeming to penetrate her very soul.

'So let's live for now. Let's live hard.'

She felt a great flowering of hope. But hope for what, she wasn't sure.

It was good to be professional again.

They saw Doris Thwaite waiting for them as they drove into the yard of High Force Farm. She looked anxious and ran towards them before they had chance to get out of the car. 'Have you seen Herbert anywhere as you drove up? Only he's gone missing.'

Jan glanced at Chris. 'No, we've not seen him. How long has he been missing for?'

Doris's voice was agitated. 'It's what he's been doing recently. He waits until my back's turned and then he sneaks out. Sometimes he just wanders around the farm. I don't mind that, but now he's started going further. And he's not safe on his feet, he came back three nights ago all cut and bruised from where he'd fallen down.'

'How long has he been gone, Doris?' Chris's voice was gentle.

'It's a couple of hours now. Longer than any time before.' Doris looked confused. 'I just can't understand how he's done it. I've hidden all his shoes—and he won't go out just wearing his slippers. How could he have got away? And where do we start looking?'

The three of them looked around. The view from the farm was immense. There were hills, ravines, woods, rock-strewn fields. Herbert could be lying injured in any one of a dozen places. 'Should we send for the mountain rescue team?' Jan asked. They'd been asked to do this kind of work before—but usually for missing children.

'Not yet,' Chris said. 'Let's think first. Doris, is there anywhere special Herbert might have gone?'

'Only around the farm. And I've been to all those places. Been to them twice.'

Chris frowned. 'People who are confused often follow old patterns of behaviour.' Jan saw the beginnings of an idea dawn in his eyes. 'He used to be a fell-runner, didn't he, Doris? Where are his old fell-running shoes?'

'He's not used them in years, they're in the back closet and I...' Doris turned and ran to her kitchen. A moment later she reappeared. 'They've gone! He must be wearing his old running shoes.'

'Right, next question. When he was training, was there any particular route around the farm that he used to follow?'

Doris smiled hopefully as she saw what he was getting at. 'There was indeed.' She turned, pointed up the hill behind the farm. 'He used to run straight up to Moses Crag there. Then he'd run along the other side of the ridge, drop down into Haven Woods and back home. It took him about an hour.'

Chris winced. 'That means it would take me about three hours.' He took off his jacket and shirt, and threw them into the back of Jan's Land Rover. 'Jan, you see to Doris here. I'll just climb up to the top of the ridge, see what I can see from there. I think following the old training run is the best hope we have. If we're out of luck then we'll have to send for more help.'

Jan eyed the muscled chest, the taut abdomen. 'I think you might finish the complete round in two hours,' she said. 'But I hope it won't be necessary.'

She took Doris's arm, led her inside. 'Don't worry,' she said. 'We'll find Herbert.'

She hoped she was telling the truth.

In fact, it was less than an hour before she saw Chris and Herbert walking down from Moses Crag, apparently talking like two old chums who hadn't met for a while.

'Herbert had just followed his old route but was having a rest on the other side of the ridge,' Chris said. 'We've had quite a chat on the way down. I wonder if I'd be any good at fell-racing.'

'Carrying a bit too much weight for a good 'un,' said Herbert. 'You need to be spare, like me.' He looked down at his feet. 'I can still move in these shoes.'

Jan looked at the set expression on Doris's face, and knew that the shoes would be confiscated—and Herbert wouldn't get them back.

'Be a good idea if you had a bath,' Chris suggested. 'Then I'll take a look at you.'

'All right, Doctor. Been nice talking to you.'

Doris hustled Herbert out of the room. 'There's a washbasin and a towel off the kitchen,' she said. 'If you want a wash, Doctor...'

'That'd be most kind. Then I can get dressed again.'

'Medicine with you is never dull, is it?' Jan asked. 'Fancy finding an old man by chasing after his running shoes.'

'It worked,' Chris said with a grin.

With some help from Doris, Herbert managed to have his bath and get dressed again. Chris examined him and then they all sat together in the kitchen and drank tea. Herbert seemed to have suffered no ill effects from his expedition. In fact, he seemed considerably better than the curmudgeon Jan remembered.

And, miraculously, he agreed to come down into town to see a consultant. 'Will you be there, Dr Garrett?'

'I certainly will,' said Chris.

'And another thing, Herbert Thwaite,' Doris said, 'if you go out again then I'm going to hang one of those bells round your neck like they put on our ewes. Then I'll know where you are.'

Herbert seemed to think this was a good idea. So, surprisingly, did Chris. 'There are these geographical signallers that let you know where a person is,' he whispered to Jan.

'They fit them to criminals. But...it would be a good idea.'

Doris decided that Herbert should go to bed. But as she passed the kitchen window she peered out and said, 'There's someone running towards the farm. Looks like a hiker. And he looks upset. He seems to be waving and I think he's shouting.'

'We'll go out and see what he wants,' said Chris. 'You put Herbert to bed.' The old man now looked a little tired after his adventure.

This was a lonely bit of country on the outskirts of the Lake District and didn't attract too many hikers. Jan and Chris went outside just as the hiker staggered into the farmyard.

He was young, about seventeen. Jan noticed that his kit was both new and expensive. 'Please, I need help. It's Harry, he fell and he's hurt and I think... We've got to call the mountain rescue or an ambulance or something. I left him and he might die.' He leaned against the wall, gasping for breath.

'Take it easy,' Chris said. 'Whatever it is, we can deal with it. I'm a doctor, this lady is a nurse and we have medical kit in the car. Now, get your breath back. Tell us your name and then tell us what happened.'

Chris's voice calmed the lad. He said, 'I'm James Baker, my friend's Harry Lang. We've been for a hike and we were messing about on this little rockface.' He pointed up the fell. 'You see, just to the side of that scree. We had no rope and Harry fell and bashed his head and I think his leg's broken.'

Jan saw Chris glance at her and received the coded message. This could be serious.

Doris had come out behind them, heard what had been said and grasped the situation at once. 'I'll settle this lad and get him a cup of tea. You do what you think is best.'

Jan took out her phone. 'I'll phone Mountain Rescue,' she said. 'They'll be here as quickly as they can, and—'

'No.' She could see that Chris was trying to come to a decision. 'Getting Mountain Rescue here might take too much time. We'll go ourselves. We have the emergency kit in the car, there's even a stretcher. Harry might be badly injured and this is the golden hour.'

She was familiar with the concept of the golden hour. After an accident, if medical workers could get to the injured person within an hour, his chances of survival were much greater. But...

'Are you sure you want to? I mean, this is specialised stuff and I—'

'Jan, I have dealt with bad falls before. More than a few. We go to see this man and if necessary phone for the ambulance or for Mountain Rescue after we have seen him.'

Jan looked at him, surprised and annoyed. This was not the old Chris, ready to discuss things with anyone. This was a man who was certain of his decision and didn't intend to have it questioned. So the words came out before she could stop them. 'You could be wrong. You've been wrong before in circumstances like these.'

She saw his face whiten as he took in what she had said, and she instantly regretted it. But he merely said, 'I have indeed. And I probably will be wrong again. It was good of you to remind me. Now, shall we get the bag and the stretcher and set off?'

They did as he suggested.

CHAPTER SIX

THEY moved up the hillside together. It was still a lovely day but Jan's mood had changed completely. She was angry at the world. More specifically, she was angry at this fallen climber, angry at Chris and most of all angry at herself. Her remark had been unnecessary and inaccurate. How stupid could she get?

She took Chris's arm, pulled him to a standstill. 'Chris. That remark was unfair, unnecessary and untrue. I'm so sorry. You're the last person in the world I want to hurt. And because I hurt you, I've hurt myself.'

He leaned forward, kissed her lightly on the forehead. 'It doesn't matter,' he said. 'We're just getting used to each other again. Now, let's move.'

They had to concentrate on following the path, angling up to where the fallen climber was lying. She was glad that Chris didn't speak—she had enough trouble with her thoughts.

They found Harry lying in the shelter of a great rock. He was half-conscious, which was a good thing as it helped him deal with the pain. There was a blood-stained scarf wrapped round his head as a rough bandage. And his leg was bent and twisted at an unnatural angle.

'Harry? You can stop worrying now, we're here to help you. I'm a doctor, Jan here is a nurse. We'll soon have you safe, warm and comfortable.'

Reassuring words, always necessary for an accident victim. If their patient felt safe he was less likely to go into shock.

Chris was lifting the edge of the scarf, peering at the gash underneath. Delicately he probed the skull around the wound. Then he grunted with what might have been satisfaction. 'Could have been a lot worse. Can you get a temporary dressing on this, Jan?'

They weren't treating Harry's injuries, just making sure that they didn't get worse until he could have the full attention of hospital staff. The head wound might well need suturing—in the proper place.

'Want to phone for an ambulance, Jan? This lad needs to get to hospital.'

Jan took out her phone, checked for a signal. They were in luck, she could get through. Ambulance Dispatch knew her—they would send an ambulance at once. But they were out in the country so it would take time.

Now Chris asked where the pain was, running his hands over the rest of Harry's body, making sure there were no injuries that had been overlooked. 'Head,' Harry mumbled. 'And my leg hurts. Please, stop it hurting.'

'We'll see what we can do. Just hang on a minute, Harry.'

Jan had taken scissors from her bag and cut away one leg of Harry's trousers so the broken leg was exposed. Then, very gently, she unlaced and took off his boot. She pinched one of his toenails. It went white—and didn't promptly go pink when she released it. She winced and looked up at Chris. 'Capillary return very poor indeed,' she said.

This was bad news. Chris was examining the leg, gently feeling where it was obvious that the bone was broken. 'Multiple closed fracture,' he said. 'And with poor capillary refill I think we have serious bleeding into the tissues. We're going to have to reduce the fracture and then get the leg into a traction splint.'

'There's a Sager splint in the bag. But should we reduce the fracture now? It would be easier when the ambulance arrives.'

'I think it has to be done now,' he said. 'Too long without capillary refill, he could lose the leg.'

'Reduction of a break like this—it's going to be difficult.'

'I've done a fair number of them. Abroad, fishermen were always getting their legs caught between their boats and the dock. Broken legs were common.'

'OK, if you feel up to doing it. He'll need morphine first. What dose do you want?' Jan reached for the syringe.

Reducing the leg wasn't a job she would have wanted. But she followed Chris's instructions, and together they got the leg straightened and at its proper length. Carefully, they fitted the Sager splint, and checked that capillary return was back to normal. 'Now let's carry him down to meet the ambulance,' Chris said.

The biggest problem once they were at the farm was persuading Doris not to feed Harry.

'This is my kitchen! I can at least get the poor lad a drink of tea.'

'He's unconscious, and he can't have anything by mouth,' Jan said. 'He'll need a general anaesthetic when he gets to hospital.'

In fact, there was little more they could do for Harry. They left him on the stretcher in the kitchen, covered him with a blanket to keep him warm and maintained a watch. His friend James watched fearfully.

'Done much rock-climbing, James?' Chris asked casually.

'Not really. In fact, none at all. We watched some fellows earlier and it looked fun. So we had a go on our own.'

'You saw they had ropes, climbing kit—they knew what they were doing?'

'I suppose so.'

'And you didn't know what you were doing. You just had a go. So what's the lesson you've learned?'

James looked uncomfortable. 'Learn to do it properly, I suppose,' he mumbled. 'Go on a course or something.'

'Good idea. Then you won't be hanging around someone's kitchen wondering if your friend is going to lose his leg.'

James went white and swallowed.

'A bit hard on him, weren't you?' Jan whispered to Chris. 'Isn't he upset enough?'

'If there's a lesson to be learned, now's the time to learn it. He'll remember.'

'I suppose so,' Jan said. She'd just seen another, tougher Chris. And she thought that perhaps she liked him.

There was nothing to do now but wait for the ambulance. Chris carefully wrote down all that they had done, all the observations he had made. Harry would soon not be his patient, and it was important that the handover was carried out correctly.

The ambulance arrived, Chris handed over his notes and then they said goodbye to Doris—who seemed to have quite enjoyed her two little bits of excitement. Then Jan and Chris headed back, too.

'Will you phone the hospital to find out how Harry is?'

'I certainly will. Though I'm certain he'll be transferred at once to Orthopaedics. I think we've both got a bit of a stake in Harry now.'

'Too right.'

There was silence for a while until she drove onto the main road. She had chosen not to take the smaller road along the river valley. Once in the day was enough.

When they were on the main road, she said, 'We've both got plenty to do at work.'

'But...?'

He had detected the hesitancy in her voice. And she was very hesitant. She was wondering where this would lead.

'But...do you fancy coming round for supper tonight? Not a full meal, I've got lots of domestic chores to do this evening. Just a drink and a sandwich at about ten?'

She felt his gaze on her, serious now. 'Yes, I do fancy coming round. Any special reason?'

She shrugged. 'Not really. We seem to be professional with each other so much. I just want to talk casually with you. An evening without an agenda. I still don't know what I'm thinking or feeling!'

After quite a while he said, 'I know what you mean about an evening without an agenda. And I think I'm quite looking forward to it.'

Then he grinned and said, 'Do you think I might kiss you again?'

'You never know your luck,' she said. She felt a glow of satisfaction, but she didn't let it show. He was coming to see her. They would be alone again. He might think he was going back to Bangladesh. But she was putting up a fight.

* * *

Through his cottage window Chris could glimpse mountains bathed in the evening sun. Just the opposite of the flat landscape he had become used to. He had thought that he'd had more than enough of mountains—but just recently the old attraction had returned.

He decided to forget about the job offer for a while and think about the evening ahead. He was looking forward to spending time with Jan. Recently they had seen a lot of each other. They had argued, climbed mountains, treated patients. He had kissed her, had even almost... It had all been exciting. He was looking forward to a gentle evening, what she had called an evening without an agenda. He just wanted to sit with her, look at her, enjoy being with her. A gentle evening. Would he kiss her at the end of it? Well, decisions could be postponed.

He set off, intending to arrive at her cottage exactly on the stroke of ten. He'd brought a bottle of red wine with him. Then it struck him that she might want something different from a gentle evening. What exactly did she want with him? He had a slightly nervous feeling of expectation.

She answered his ring promptly, smiled at him. Even though it had been only a short time since he had said goodbye to her, his heart thumped with excitement. Like him she was dressed casually, her thin shirt and cotton trousers emphasising an athletic but undoubtedly feminine body.

He wondered whether to kiss her—not a full-blooded kiss on the lips but a chaste salute on each cheek, as a guest might give to his hostess. Then he decided not to. For the moment, all kissing was a minefield. But later...

He gave her the bottle of wine. She led him to a seat on

her lounge then took the bottle away to open it. Eventually she came to sit across from him, handed him a glass of wine and raised her own in salute.

She gave him a smile that made his heart thump again. 'You said you'd phone up about Harry. How is he?'

'Harry is good. They took one look at him in A and E, sent him straight over to Orthopaedics. The surgeon operated at once, I got to talk to him afterwards. We made the right decision, setting that leg. With any luck and plenty of physio, the lad won't even have a limp. And he could have lost the leg.'

'Or worse,' she said. 'And *we* didn't make a decision. You did.'

He shrugged. 'I felt glad that you were there,' he said.

She sipped her wine. 'You're a very good emergency doctor now, aren't you?'

'I've had a lot of practice.'

'And you're good with people, too.'

'We all learn.'

'You're not the man I knew six years ago.'

'I'm older and heavier, possibly wiser and sadder.'

'And what's this about you not liking mountains? I could tell the minute you stepped out of the car, the way you looked at the skyline—the old attraction is back.'

'I'm afraid it is,' he admitted. 'And when I think of mountains, I think of you. And when I think of you I think of…'

'Let me guess. Mountains. You're easy to read, Dr Garrett. Now, let me pour you another glass of wine. And I've got some nibbles in the kitchen.'

He looked down, amazed that he had finished his first drink.

She smiled as she went into the kitchen. It was fun pretending that they were just friends, having an idle conversation. But there was more to it. If he thought he was going back to Bangladesh without a fight—for another six years? She'd have to prove to him that England had plenty to offer.

She returned to the living room, placed bowls of nuts and crisps on the table, then, in a noncommittal voice, she managed to ask, 'Have you thought any more about the job offer? Are you going back abroad?' She hoped her voice was as casual as she intended it to be.

He looked at her carefully. 'Possibly,' he said. 'But I've got a month in which to decide. I must say, England seems a lot more inviting now.'

Would he, please, say why it was more inviting? She didn't dare ask.

'When I knew you...before,' she said, 'you wanted to be a GP. Why did you change your mind?'

Her head had been bent as she'd asked the question, but as she finished it she looked up, stared into his eyes. And then she shivered at the sad way he was looking back at her.

He took some time before answering. Finally, deliberately, he said, 'I realised I was very young. I wasn't really mature enough to be a GP. A good GP is a counsellor as well as a doctor. Academically I was gifted, I was well trained, but I knew nothing about life.'

'From what you've told me, you know about life now.' She decided to be daring. 'You do know that your uncle would be overjoyed if you offered to become his partner?'

Chris grinned. 'He hasn't asked me,' he said. 'But it's not hard to guess what he's thinking. And I must say, I—'

Someone rang her doorbell. She could only sit there, wondering what the odd sound was. The she realised and glanced at her watch. It was late for a call.

'Shall I answer it?' Chris asked. She shook her head, but noticed that he accompanied her to the door.

'Community Nurse Fielding? And perhaps Dr Garrett?'

Jan looked at the caller, her eyes unfocussed, her thoughts many miles away. What did this man want? Couldn't he tell that she had important things to think about?'

Chris spoke first. 'I'm Dr Garrett and, yes, this is Community Nurse Fielding. Can we help you?'

Jan looked at the man more closely. He was tall, held himself erect, had a clipped moustache. She suspected his suit had cost more than she earned in a couple months.

'Might I speak with you for a minute? I know it's late and I don't want to spoil your evening, but I really would like a quick word. And let me say first I'm not trying to sell you anything.'

Chris smiled, extended his hand. 'I recognise your face,' he said, 'or, to be exact, I recognise your son's face. You're Harry's father.'

The minute Chris said it, Jan saw the resemblance. 'Please, do come in, sit down a minute,' she said. 'Perhaps you'd like a glass of wine? You must have had a rough day.'

The man shook Chris's hand, turned and offered his hand to Jan. 'I have indeed had a rough day, but the end of it has been—well, better than the beginning. And I felt I just couldn't rest until I'd tried to thank the people who made that ending possible. As to the glass of wine, I feel like a teenager going to a party. I've brought my own bottle.' From somewhere the man produced a bottle of champagne. 'Might I ask you to share this with me?'

Jan knew nothing about champagne. But Chris obviously did, and Jan felt like giggling when she saw the expression of consternation on his face as he saw the label.

'Take our guest through, Chris,' she said, 'and I'll fetch some champagne glasses.'

The two glasses and the bottle of red wine were put to one side. Jan gave her champagne glasses a quick wipe and rub and Chris neatly popped the cork and poured. Three glasses of champagne bubbled on the coffee-table.

'I'm Henry, Lord Grayleigh,' the man said. 'And this morning you saved the leg, possibly the life, of my oldest son.'

Jan blinked. She'd heard of this man, but had never met him. He was the largest landowner for miles around, and many of the local farmers were his tenants. He had a good reputation for trying to stop the drift from the countryside— he had built cheap houses for sale to locals only, had endowed a wing in the local college of further education. And she'd helped save the life of his son!

'We phoned to find out how he was,' Chris said. 'He seemed to be doing well.'

'I've just left the hospital, come straight here. Had a long conversation with the orthopaedic consultant. He said if you hadn't reduced the leg at once, with bleeding into the tissues—consequences could have been quite bad.'

Chris shrugged. 'Perhaps. We're a doctor and a nurse, we were handy and we were pleased to do what we could.'

Lord Grayleigh nodded. 'Thought you'd say something like that. However...' He pushed a glass of champagne over to each of them and took up his own glass. Formally, he said, 'Nurse Fielding and Dr Garrett, I suspect you saved the life of my son. I couldn't envisage life without him—though life with him is sometimes a bit trying. You have the thanks of my wife, myself and, indeed, Harry. Here's to you both.'

There was just a small quaver in his voice and as he lifted his glass, Jan realised just how deeply moved the man was. She wondered for a moment what it would be like to lose a child. Would it be worse than losing a parent? And that thought made her blanch.

She sipped the wine offered her—then sipped again. This was not the usual Spanish sparkling wine that she occasionally drank and enjoyed so much. This was something very, very different. And she very much liked it.

'I see you are together this evening,' Lord Grayleigh went on in a more controlled voice. 'I phoned your uncle, Dr Garrett, to find out where you might be—he gave me your two addresses. You weren't at home so I came here and it's good to find you together. Are you just colleagues or...?'

'Just colleagues,' Jan said firmly. She wondered if she should add, 'for the moment, anyway'.

'And we are good friends,' Chris added.

'I see. Nurse Fielding, I gather you are settled in here, intend to stay.'

'I was born here, I love it and I wouldn't dream of leaving. This is my home.'

'Good, good. Dr Garrett, your uncle must be near retirement. Are you going to stay with us?'

Jan felt a pang as Chris shook his head. 'I'm not sure. I've just been offered a job abroad that...well, it's very inviting. In Bangladesh.'

'Bangladesh?' Lord Grayleigh said. 'Well...that'll be different.'

Jan had a job to stop herself from laughing. Obviously Lord Grayleigh was not enthused by Bangladesh.

They chatted for a while longer, and then Lord Grayleigh said that he'd better go, his wife was just getting over the shock and he was quite tired himself. 'I won't insult you by offering you money, but if there's any—'

'A contribution to the mountain rescue team would be welcome,' Chris said. 'We're both enthusiastic members of the team.'

'An excellent idea. I can't think of a better one. Have you the address of the secretary or treasurer?' Jan fetched him the address and Lord Grayleigh stood and shook hands with them both again. 'I do hope we meet again soon. In fact, I'm sure we will. Dr Garrett, it would be lovely if you stayed with us.'

They escorted him to the door, saw a long dark car with a chauffeur waiting for him by the gate. Lord Grayleigh travelled in style.

'We're heroes,' Chris said when they sat down again.

'I rather like it. You know, this evening's not been what I expected. I invited you here so we could have a quiet couple of hours together. But with Lord Grayleigh turning up, it just hasn't happened.'

'So. Shall we be quiet now?'

'That would be lovely. I don't want to have any more serious conversations for a while. Let's just finish the champagne.'

'A great idea.'

The champagne was to blame, of course. Jan wasn't used to it and she'd had a hard day before drinking it. They finished the rest of the bottle—and Lord Grayleigh had only had one small glass.

Eventually Chris stood. 'It's late,' he said. 'I should be getting home.'

He looked at her and unspoken messages flew between them. And it was she who decided. Not yet. Probably soon.

But she walked him to the door and it was inevitable that he should kiss her, and it was just as shattering to her as it had been the previous time.

'What are we going to do?' she asked. 'Sweetheart, you're giving me something I just couldn't give up.'

He seemed to be lost for an answer. Eventually he said, 'I don't know what we'll do. But we'll have to do something.'

'Kiss me again while you're thinking.'

CHAPTER SEVEN

SHE tried not to think after he'd gone. She undressed and washed, prepared her usual mug of cocoa and drank it in her usual way, curled up on the couch. Then she went to bed. But she couldn't sleep. While she was doing things she could avoid wondering about what had happened—what was happening to her. But once in bed the thoughts came unbidden and nothing she could do would banish them.

What was she to do about Chris? She had found out that they had misjudged each other all these years. She thought that perhaps—in time—they might get together and... But he was going back to Bangladesh! Jan just didn't know what to think. She lay on her back, on her side, sat up to plump out her pillows, kicked the bedclothes off and then dragged them back on again.

She had enjoyed their evening. She had intended to probe a little, to find out what his feelings about her were, to try to discover if they had any kind of future. She wanted to get things settled between them. But that hadn't happened. The arrival of Lord Grayleigh had put serious thoughts well out of her mind. And it made her feel good, to be so frankly appreciated.

So how did she feel now?

Eventually she got up. A quick glance out of her bedroom window showed it was still dark, but there was the lightening in the east that showed that dawn wasn't too far away. She felt lonely, desolate. Wasn't this the time when human spirits were at their lowest?

Would she make her own spirits even lower?

It was in the bottom drawer of the chest that was in the spare bedroom. The key to the drawer was at the back of her bedside cabinet—no way was she going to lose it.

She took the key, opened the drawer, drew aside the blankets folded on top and took out a folder. There had been a time when she had gone through this ritual two or three times a week—but now she realised she hadn't opened the drawer for nearly a month. Did that prove anything?

She sat at her kitchen table and opened the folder. On the top there was an article, cut out of the local newspaper. The headline was 'Hillside Death of Local Farmer'. The large picture was of her father. It was one that she had supplied, a favourite picture showing her father as she remembered him, a strong, smiling man with the background of the fells that he loved.

It was part article, part obituary. She practically knew it by heart now. Details of her father's life, a well-respected local farmer—family been in valley for generations, founder and leader of the mountain rescue team. Survived by one daughter, Janice Fielding. Then the account of his death and the coroner's verdict—misadventure. And that was that.

She sat and waited for the vision to come. Two faces. First of all her father's face, relaxed in death. Then Chris's face, looking much younger than it did now. And he looked horrified, and as frightened as she felt. She had seen it so often.

The vision didn't come.

She smiled to herself. She had half known it before, now she was certain. The past was dead. All there was between Chris and her now was the future. Carefully she put away the folder, knowing it would be months before she looked at it again. She went to her bed and slept at once.

He came to her cottage for supper again the next night. She liked that. They were getting to be at ease with each other. This was a new relationship, an adult relationship, and they were cautious about it.

She sat with him in her living room, this time drinking tea rather than wine. 'I want to talk about something different. Tell me about the work you've been doing for the past six years. Did you like it? Was it what you expected?'

He thought a moment. 'It wasn't what I expected. I went out there as a young, innocent, inexperienced doctor, intending to do good. And very quickly I discovered that any good I could do was outweighed by the good I couldn't do.'

'So you didn't like it?'

He shook his head. 'I made a lot of friends. And I know that quite a few babies have survived because of me, quite a lot of people are healthier because of me. I even saved a few lives. But sometimes the sheer size of the problem gets on top of you. You can never do enough. And if you're working on some kind of a disaster site—can you imagine how hard it is to eat something, knowing that not two miles or twenty minutes away, there's someone whose life could be saved by that food?'

She thought a moment. 'I can imagine,' she said, 'though it's horrible. What do you do?'

'You keep eating. You remind yourself that you're more good to people alive than you are dead. And you need the food to stay alive.'

'I see. Now tell me the good bits.'

'It can be very beautiful, especially in the early morning. To see a great expanse of water, mists rising from it—it's wonderful. I know you like mountains, and I'm coming back round to that way of thinking myself, but flatness can have its beauty.'

'I'll take your word for it. But for me the landscape needs to be bumpy in order to be interesting.' She was relaxing more now, enjoying his company. They seemed to have slipped into a state in which their previous lives were forgotten. For now there was only the two of them sitting here, chatting idly, pleased to be together.

'On Sunday,' he said, 'I thought of going on a flat walk that I've heard about. Would you like to come with me? I'm missing large sheets of water. Perhaps you'll see the beauty, too.'

She frowned. 'The forecast is that the weather won't be too good on Sunday. It's going to be unsettled. That means it's going to be misty, there'll be some light rain.'

'All to the good. Mist and flat water are a great combination.'

'Where exactly are you taking me?'

'Wait and see. It'll be worth it.'

She was feeling sleepy now. She hadn't slept well the night before, had worked a full day, prepared for the evening and eaten a large meal. Her eyelids were heavy. Surely it wouldn't hurt to close them just for a minute. He could carry on talking. So she closed her eyes, listening vaguely to him talking about rice paddies.

She seemed to be sliding sideways a little. Half-consciously she noticed that there was an arm round her, comforting and comfortable. No problem there. Rice paddies were really, truly fascinating…

When she woke it was dark. She was perfectly comfortable and the arm around her still held her close. She could smell some citrusy aftershave, feel the swell of his breathing and under that feel the warmth of his body. It was…it was nice.

She felt her own body come half-awake. And with the awakening came feelings she had not known for many years. But they were good feelings. She was enjoying them.

Still half-asleep, she mumbled something, stretched a lethargic arm around him and pulled him closer. His head came down towards hers. I'm not fully awake, she told herself, not responsible. I can get away with things because I don't know what I'm doing, so there's no need to think of any consequences.

He kissed her. Gently at first, tentatively, as if not sure of her reaction. She wasn't sure of her reaction either. But…she guessed she liked it. It made her feel warm and comfortable and needed and protected. She didn't exactly kiss him back. But somehow she made it obvious that she didn't mind.

Of course, they couldn't carry on like this for ever. They'd be stopping soon. But, just for now, as his grip on her tightened and when her lips opened of their own accord, and when she felt him closer, and more demanding…she just had to agree, didn't she? Besides, she was liking it so much.

They were a bit cramped. It was hard for him to lean over her, hard for her to reach right round his twisted body. She may as well lie down on the couch—it was big enough. And he could bend over her. So she wriggled a bit, lifted up her legs and—yes, that was better.

He thought so, too, she could tell by his sigh of excitement. And when he kissed her this time she was completely awake—but she had lost all interest in consequences. What was happening now was all that mattered.

She felt his hand slide under the loose edge of her shirt, and he started to stroke her midriff. His fingertips were so soft. She knew that he could feel her breathing, perfectly in time with his.

His fingers moved upwards, touched the underside of her half-cup bra. She muttered something that even she didn't understand, then moved so that he could slip a hand round her back, unhook her bra. Then she jerked in a spasm of delight as his fingers caressed her now erect breasts.

It was her turn. She didn't want to be simply passive. She reached inside his shirt, rubbed against the cords of muscle, detected the rapid beating of his heart. Beating rapidly, like her own.

Things now seemed to be happening with their own inevitability. It wasn't that she didn't want them to happen—she was so happy that they did. Just that she didn't remember making any definite decision.

With an almost vague surprise she discovered that both their shirts were discarded, that he was lying next to her, almost on her. Her breasts were crushed to his chest, she was kissing him with an abandon that was matched by his. Perhaps they should move now, go upstairs to her bedroom and… What was that ringing?

She tried to ignore it, what she was doing now was far

more important than any telephone call. And when she moved, Chris's grip on her tightened. 'Let it ring,' he muttered. 'Whoever it is, they'll soon go away.'

But she couldn't let it ring, and she knew that neither could he. They were both programmed. Late-night calls tended to be about emergencies, and they had to be answered.

She moved to sit up and he released her at once. Before she crossed the room to her phone, she picked up her shirt and draped it around her shoulders. There seemed to be something vaguely improper about a community nurse answering the phone with nothing on above the waist.

'Hello, Jan. It's Penny here. I've just got your message on my answering machine. Sorry I'm late, I've been out to the college. Is this a good time to call? You're not on your way to bed or anything?'

Jan smiled weakly, glancing at Chris. 'No, I'm not on my way to bed,' she said, 'but it won't be long now. Nothing special, Penny. I just thought I might call round tomorrow evening and wondered if you'd be in.'

'I'm in all evening. Will you come to tea?'

'Thanks but no. I've got a couple of late visits. I'll come round at about eight.'

'Looking forward to seeing you.' Penny rang off.

Chris hadn't moved from the couch. She walked over to sit next to him, picked up his hands and kissed them. 'We nearly...' she said.

'We nearly,' he agreed. 'I wanted to so much and so did you. Perhaps if we...?'

She shook her head. 'I'm sorry, really sorry, but I just couldn't. I'm frightened now. When...if...we do, then I want to be certain about things.'

'Things?' His voice was low, but there was just that touch of humour in it.

'You're not disappointed in me? You don't think I led you on and then...?'

This time it was he who took her hands, raised them to her lips. 'You could never disappoint me.'

'Chris, I wanted to so much. But I've got used to bottling my feelings up. If we had gone on then, if Penny hadn't phoned, then it would have been fine. But now there's a mean little fear inside me that says I've got to stay cool and logical and not make myself vulnerable any more. And—you might leave me. I couldn't stand that. Do you understand?'

'I understand.' She thought she could feel his sadness but she knew that he did truly understand. He let go of her hands. She couldn't help it, she had to pull her shirt more tightly round her.

She knew that this sudden tearing apart was hurting him just as much as it was hurting her and she had to admire his self-control. 'Shall I go?' he asked, after the silence between them had stretched to unendurable lengths.

She was tempted to say no. But cold common sense came to her rescue and she said, 'Perhaps you'd better. And for what it's worth, I'm sorry for leading you on.'

'I don't know who led who on. Perhaps a bit of both.' He was pulling on his shirt, reaching for his jacket. 'Are we still all right for our walk on Sunday?' She saw he was smiling, and there was a wry amusement in his voice as he went on, 'We'll be out in the cold and the wet and the open air.'

'We should be all right there,' she agreed with a smile. 'Good night, Chris.'

'Night, Jan.'

She didn't move as he left the room, just listened for the snap of the front door closing, the gentle roar of his car engine. Then she remained perfectly still for ten minutes. She tried to think, but her thoughts were confused. What was she doing, what did she want?

There was no answer, so she went to bed.

'I once read that the Chinese, or some people anyway, believe that if you save a person's life, then you are obliged to look after them for the rest of the life that you have saved,' Penny said. 'Have you ever heard that?'

'Something like it,' Jan said. 'I suppose it means that a lot of doctors and nurses have a lot of looking-after to do.' She and Penny were sitting on Penny's patio again, drinking tea with the sweet-smelling roses over their heads. 'What makes you wonder about that?'

Penny smiled wryly. 'I'm getting older now so I can shout my own praises without blushing. Last time you were here, with Chris, I took a chance, I interfered with your lives. And now I want to make sure that I did the right thing. I'm looking after you. Did I do the right thing?'

Jan was quiet a moment. Then she admitted, 'You certainly did. But it was a bit of a shock. We needed our heads knocked together.'

'Perhaps you did. But people learn from their mistakes. Are you happier now? And how is Chris?'

'We're both much happier now. But there's still a long way to go. What we had all those years ago has gone—it can't and it shouldn't be started again. We're new people now. We're finding each other again.'

'Is it fun?'

'It's fun but at times it's difficult,' Jan confessed. 'And there's a big problem. He's been offered this wonder job back in Bangladesh. He half wants to accept it and he feels he ought to do it.'

'You wouldn't go with him?'

Jan sighed. 'Well, he hasn't asked me, has he? But he knows that no matter how I tried, I'd only end up making him miserable there.'

'You've grown up,' Penny said laconically. 'You wouldn't have made that hard-headed remark six years ago. Do you love him?'

Jan thought. She wanted to be absolutely clear about this—both for herself and to be honest to Penny.

'I could love him,' she said. 'I think he could love me, too. Though he's never said so. Not this time.'

Penny stood and said, 'Pour yourself some more tea. There's something I want to show you.' Her voice was unusually terse, and Jan wondered if she'd upset her friend. But how?

Five minutes later Penny was back. On the table she laid a leather-covered photograph album. Although strong-looking, it was worn and had obviously been much handled.

'You know I trained in Sheffield in the late 1950s,' Penny said. 'Then I came back home here to work. Well, these are a few photographs of my time there.'

Jan looked at her curiously. 'I'm fascinated. Why have you never shown me these before?'

'Look inside and you'll find out.'

So Jan looked inside. There were black-and-white photographs of a much younger Penny—and she had been gorgeous in her time. Penny pointed to one picture. 'Me in my bikini at the outdoor baths in Scarborough. I felt very dashing—and very nervous.'

'You look...sexy,' Jan said.

Penny laughed. 'I was,' she said. 'For those days I was a very...outgoing girl.'

Jan continued to turn the pages. 'Who's this young man you're with? Look, he's got you on the pillion of his motorbike!'

'His name was David Miller. Dr David Miller. We were together for two years. Just after I passed my finals he asked me to marry him, we'd get a flat in Sheffield. I said I wouldn't marry him, not yet, that I wanted to live a little first. I came home to be with my parents. He came up here to see me, and on the way here he crashed that motorbike and was killed.'

Jan couldn't help it. Her eyes filled with tears. 'Oh, poor you,' she said. 'Penny, I'm so sorry. And you've looked at these pictures through the years?'

'Just me. And it hasn't done me much good.'

Jan thought of her own concealed folder, and shivered. 'You showed me these photographs for a reason, didn't you?' she asked.

'I did. I didn't have a second chance. You have.'

'I see,' said Jan.

'Typical Lakeland weather,' she said. 'One thing you can count on here is that you can count on the worst weather possible will be where you want to walk.' She pulled up the hood of her anorak. 'Unsettled means mist and rain.'

It was the following Sunday. They were standing on the beach at Arnside, looking across the flat sands and meandering watercourses of Morecambe Bay. 'Grange over Sands is somewhere over there in the mist,' she went on. 'Let's hope we find it.'

At the moment there was no land to be seen.

There were other groups huddled round them, perhaps a hundred people altogether. Then a general movement out onto the sands, following a confident-looking guide.

'I looked up about this crossing,' Chris told her. 'Apparently there's been a guide across these sands for hundreds of years. The one we've got now is still paid for by the Crown. People have been killed trying to cross on their own.'

'I always tell people that a good guide is worth it. Come on, let's get started.'

This was a different kind of walking. In fact, most of the time it was paddling. They had their boots tied round their necks, trousers rolled up to the knees, an ancient pair of trainers each. Sometimes there was sand underfoot, sometimes sand covered with a couple inches of water, sometimes the water was deeper. And then it started to drizzle.

Occasionally the guide would ask them to stop so he could check the way or make sure that the sand wasn't too dangerous. It was on one of these stops that Jan really looked around. They were up to their knees in water. It was raining, a thin, fine rain. The coast had disappeared, and there was no sign of land anywhere, just mist and water as far as the eye could see. And the little group waiting patiently with no idea where land or safety were.

'Are you enjoying this?' Chris asked.

She thought a minute. 'I'm loving it,' she said after a while. 'Largely because it's different. But what is it like if this is all you can see, day after day after day?'

'It can get a bit tedious,' he admitted. 'But after a while you don't notice. The landscape—or waterscape—just doesn't register. Look. We're moving on.'

After a while they saw a dim line ahead, which turned into the coast. It seemed odd, after the desolation they had experienced, to see houses, gardens, shops.

Although it was a Sunday, they both had things to do that afternoon. Chris had a meeting with his uncle; Jan had to organise a list of supplies she was going to need. What had been intended to be a day together had turned out just to be a morning. But he had wanted to come, and so had she.

They returned to their cars and stood on the road, looking at the expanse of sand and sea that they had just crossed. 'Why did you want to bring me here?' she asked.

'I'm not sure. I wanted to give you some idea of what my life used to be like. What I saw first thing in the morning.'

'It's a lonely landscape. Did it make you lonely?'

'No. It made me more…self-contained.'

'I can understand that.'

They both stared outwards, not looking at each other. Then he said, 'Now it's hard for me to be open with people. To tell them what I think and I feel. Sometimes it's hard to admit to myself what I'm feeling. I've taught myself to do without emotions. That way you don't get hurt.'

'It'll come,' she said. 'Give it time, give it a chance, and it'll come.'

She didn't want to part from him. And there was only one thing she could think of to ask him. 'You say you need to be more open with people. But if you take this job back in Bangladesh, won't you need to be like you were before? Won't you need to be self-contained again?'

He was silent for so long that she thought he wasn't going to answer her. But eventually he said, 'Yes. I shall need to be self-contained again. In fact, since I'll be in a position of greater responsibility, I'll need to be more self-contained than ever.'

'I see.' She had to ask. 'So you'd be so self-contained that there'd be no place for me?'

He sighed. 'I can't even think about that.'

CHAPTER EIGHT

ON MONDAY morning Chris knocked, put his head round her consulting-room door.

'It's nice to be wanted,' he said, 'and we're both wanted.'

Can't you tell that we want each other? Jan thought, but only said, 'Who wants us?'

'There's to be a big charity ball at Lord Grayleigh's house next weekend. He's sent us two tickets, says would we, please, come as his guests. Would you like to go? If you aren't doing anything.'

'Yes,' she said. 'I've heard of these balls and I'd love to go to one.'

'It'll be posh,' he said with a grin. 'In fact, it will be super posh. You in your best ball gown and me in my penguin suit.'

'It'll be hard deciding which of my many ball gowns to wear. But I'll force myself to make a decision.'

'Good. I'll send a formal acceptance from both of us.'

And he was gone.

Jan was elated by the invitation but just a little irritated by Chris's diffidence. Surely he must know she wanted to go with him? Why was he always so ready to leave her a way out? By now, he ought to know that she was interested in him. Couldn't he presume on that—just a little?

Then the cold thought struck her. Perhaps he was being fair to her. Perhaps he was keeping her at a distance because he had already made up his mind to go abroad and didn't want to let her down. Jan shivered.

She glanced at her watch. Her first patient would arrive in five minutes. That was good: it would stop her thinking and worrying about other things. Such as, why was her heart thumping so?

The last formal occasion she had gone to had been with her ex-fiancé, Peter Harris. And that had been two years ago. Before that she couldn't remember the last time she'd been to a proper, dressed-up, must-look-your-best ball. And that decided her. It might be just once. But she would make going to Lord Grayleigh's ball an occasion to remember.

She knew that all the richest and most distinguished of the county would be at this dance. It would be formal. Very formal. Ladies would be wearing the family jewels. Jan didn't have any family jewels. But—she stuck her jaw out—she would do as well. She would show Chris that she didn't have to wear a nurse's uniform, or climbing gear, or casual jeans and T-shirt. If necessary, she could dress up as well as anyone.

She managed to arrange an afternoon off work, and drove up to Carlisle with a list of boutiques to visit. It wasn't something that she did very often and after a while she found it was very enjoyable. The first place had something that would do perfectly—but was just out of her budget range: a long dress in a white silvery fabric, slit down each side. There was hardly any back, and two straps supported a very low-cut front. It matched her hair, her skin colour. She looked so good in it.

But…it was very expensive. She sighed and hung it back on its rail.

There were other dresses that she very much liked but none that spoke to her, none that said, *You've just got to have me.* So she went to the next shop and looked further. In all, she visited six shops and bought nothing. She got tired of wriggling in and out of dresses, so she went for a coffee and treated herself to a cream cake.

The treat revived her, and it became obvious what she had to do. Go back to the first shop and buy the silvery white dress. So she did just that.

'New underwear, madam?' the sales assistant said. She viewed Jan's serviceable bra with some scorn. 'We can't really wear that bra with this dress, can we?'

'We can't,' Jan agreed. She was directed to a bra that gave her a whole new—but very attractive—shape, and a matching wispy pair of knickers that would never keep her warm on a mountainside. No tights, but a pair of silver stay-ups with hearts on the top.

One more place to visit, but this turned out to be easy. She found the silver shoes she needed within minutes of entering the shop.

She drove home much poorer but much happier. By her side was a large shiny scarlet box, with her silver dress inside it.

'I hope you've got a really smart dinner jacket,' she told Chris the next morning when they met in the staff lounge. 'I'm not going with a man who smells of mothballs. I've spent a fortune on my dress.'

'Just to go with me?'

'Just to go to the ball. I want to look smart.'

He laughed. 'I'll try not to let you down. In fact, there were towns near where I used to work that were very good for clothing. But you'll see. Incidentally, Lord Grayleigh has been in touch and has arranged to have us picked up and taken back in one of his cars. We'll arrive and leave in style.'

'As always,' she said.

There was a pause and then she said, 'I think this evening is going to be important. For both of us.'

He caught her meaning at once. 'I see,' he said gravely. 'You've been thinking about the future?'

'I've been thinking a lot,' she said, 'and it's time I got on with my life. It's time you got on with your life. I'd like to think that this ball represented a turning point for both of us.'

And in that case she might as well do the job completely. On Saturday morning she booked herself a hair appointment, a manicure and a facial. And as she sat there under the drier, she wondered at herself. She didn't feel like a girl going to a Cinderella-type ball. Rather she felt like someone about to do battle—and she was. But the battle wasn't with Chris. The battle was with herself. Only she could make herself happy.

She might have guessed how smart Chris would be. But when he turned up on her doorstep, she was amazed. He was wearing the classic men's dinner jacket. Single-breasted shawl collar, tiny diamond studs in the shirtfront, an obviously hand-tied bow-tie. It was summer and it was hot, so he was entitled to wear a white jacket. A single crimson rose in his buttonhole. And the fabric was... 'What's your suit made of?' she asked.

'It's silk,' he told her. 'Silk of various thicknesses. Just the thing you need, either to keep cool or keep warm.'

'It looks very classy. I like it.'

Now he looked at her. 'I need to be classy if I'm with you. That dress is wonderful. Jan, I think you'll be the most beautiful woman at the ball.'

He was absolutely sincere, she could feel it. And his words made her feel wanted and excited and…and she wasn't quite sure what else. 'Come in for a moment,' she said. He had phoned that afternoon, arranged to come to her house and said the car would pick them up there.

From behind his back he produced a bouquet of flowers. Roses—her favourite flower, in white, red, peach and pink. 'I brought you these, he said. 'I remembered how you liked roses. I hope you still do.'

'Oh, I do,' she said. 'And these are glorious. Sit down a minute while I put them in water.'

She fetched three vases, placed the flowers on her coffee-table.

'Thank you for these,' she said, 'They are truly lovely. Now, stand quite still while I kiss you on the cheek. I've gone to a lot of trouble with this make-up and I don't want it spoiled.'

'You're beautiful with or without make-up,' he said, and once again she thrilled at the compliment.

She kissed him on the cheek. 'I've made my mind up,' she said. 'This is going to be a fairy-tale night. I'm Cinderella going to the ball and you, believe it or not, are Prince Charming. At the end of the ball it's back to rags for me. But until then I don't want to think about the outside world. Tonight is to be a night apart.'

He nodded. 'That's fine by me. Though, I must say, Lord Grayleigh makes a funny fairy queen.'

'There's a large car just drawn up outside,' she said. 'But it'll do for a crystal coach.'

She knew it was an evening she would remember for the rest of her life. They sat in leather seats as the car purred its way to Grayleigh Castle. They joined a large queue of expensive cars but didn't need to have their invitations checked by security. The car was recognised.

They entered the great hall, their names were announced, and they were greeted by Lord and Lady Grayleigh.

'Enjoy yourselves,' Lord Grayleigh whispered. 'I'll be round for a personal word later.'

Lady Grayleigh just said, 'Thank you for what you did for my son,' then added, 'You look gorgeous in that lovely dress, my dear.' Jan didn't know which remark made her more happy.

They were given a glass of champagne and went to sit outside on the terrace, where a young man limped over and smiled shyly at them. 'Nurse Fielding, Dr Garrett? So glad you could come.' He was tall, dressed in a well-cut dinner jacket, and Jan didn't recognise him at first.

'Good to see you, Harry,' said Chris. 'How's the leg?'

Harry! The son of Lord Grayleigh and the reason they were here tonight.

'The leg is mending,' Harry said. 'I'm in a cast, I'm still limping and I won't be doing much dancing. But I'm doing the physio, and the therapist says that with any luck there'll be no serious consequences. May I sit down? I wanted to have a chat with you about something else. I'd like you to help me.'

'Whatever we can do,' said Chris.

Harry had taken his examinations and had been offered a

place at university. But he wanted to take a gap year to see something of the world. 'I've got no skills whatsoever,' he said honestly. 'Well, I'm pretty good with computers, but that's it. Still, I wondered if I could be any use in a place like Bangladesh.'

'It's a different life from all this,' Chris said, waving his arm at the house behind them.

'I know that. That's why I want a change.'

'You'll get that all right. Are you sure you won't get fed up after a few weeks? Miss the idle, easy life?'

'I'm sure I'll do both. But I'll stick at it. Will you tell me what I can expect?'

So Chris told him, and Jan listened—and sometimes shuddered. After ten minutes, Chris said, 'Are you still interested.'

'Yes,' Harry said.

Chris looked at him a while, then took out a card from his wallet. 'Write to this man and tell him what you want to do, what skills you have. I'll write to him, too, recommending you to him.'

'That's great! Thank you both so much. Now, got to do the family bit and circulate among the guests.' He smiled nervously at Jan and said, 'Nurse Garrett, if there's a slow dance later, would you take the floor for a minute with a young man with an injured leg? It would make all my friends tremendously jealous.'

'I'd love to,' Jan said with a grin. 'I've always fancied younger men.'

'Now I'm jealous,' Chris said as Harry walked away. 'Are you sure you can't fancy a middle aged man?'

'I could try with a youngish middle-aged man.'

And after that it was all magic. They ate, they danced, they chatted. They talked to Lord and Lady Grayleigh; she had her dance with Harry. 'Enjoying yourself?' Chris asked.

'You know I am. I feel we're in a separate world, in never-never land. I wouldn't want to live here all the time. But for a while I'm here and I'm with you and that's all that matters.'

'Let's have another dance,' he said. 'Or...it's dark now. We can go out on the terrace again and no one will notice that I'm kissing you.'

'We can do both,' she said.

Fairy stories had to end. But she was quite content when they decided that it was time that they left. They were driven back to her cottage in the Bentley and found themselves in her front room.

'Things don't stop at midnight in this fairy-tale,' she told him. 'I've decided. It's magic time until tomorrow morning. Then we can talk.'

'I'll come round to see you.'

She looked at him.

'Or I could stay,' he said.

There was a moment's perfect silence and then she said, 'You've looked great in that suit and I've felt lovely in this dress. But I don't want to be formal any more.'

They were standing, facing each other. They hadn't touched since they'd entered her home. She turned so her back was to him. 'Will you unzip my dress, please?' she asked.

She felt his fingers trail down the back of her neck, shuddered with delight at the lightness of the touch. The buzz of the zip going down seemed to last for ever. For a moment she clutched the front to her. Then she shrugged and the dress cascaded downwards. She stood there a moment, then stepped out of it and stooped to pick it up.

For a moment she was anxious. Her newly bought underwear was very flimsy, very revealing. But wasn't that what she wanted? She turned, and he was looking at her. When she lifted her eyes to look at him, she could feel the passion burning there. But as yet he didn't reach out to touch her.

She knew that he would. When the time was right.

'You are so lovely,' he said. His voice sounded odd. It was casual, almost detached. And that made what he said more sincere.

'I'm going to have a bath,' she told him. 'You can come in to see me if you want.'

'I do want! I want desperately but, Jan, is this part of—?'

'You say this is something that you want, and I want it, too. Or perhaps we both need it. Tomorrow will be different; tomorrow we have to decide things. But now is now. So come into the bathroom in about ten minutes.'

'Yes,' he said.

She took her dress and went upstairs, moving as if all had been decided and things were now out of her control. She hung up the dress, slipped out of her underwear and went to the bathroom, taking four large candles with her—she had always loved candles. One on each corner of the bath, so there was no need for any other light. The room filled with steam. She shook in an expensive bath oil and then slid into the water.

After a while there was a knock on the door, she called him to come in. He had taken off his jacket and his tie, and to her he looked more handsome than ever. He seemed to loom through the clouds of steam, the candlelight making his face a mask of shapes and shadows. 'I'm undressed,' she said. 'Why aren't you?'

'Is there room in there for two?'

She ran her fingers across the surface of the water, making ripples that lapped against the side of the bath. 'Well, actually, yes,' she said. 'I wanted a big bath so I ordered one.'

He looked at her for a minute and then walked to her bedroom.

Perhaps she was shy—no, she couldn't be shy, she'd just undressed in front of him, let him see her naked in the bath. Still, when he came back into the bathroom, she didn't look at him. She gazed at the candle at the far end of the bath as if there were secrets to be deciphered in its flickering flame.

He said nothing. She felt a foot by her side in the bath, then he levered himself in to sit facing her. The water level rose, and she felt it lap against her breasts. Only then did she look at him.

A broad chest, two waves of dark hair spreading across it. Muscular shoulders that curved down easily to equally muscular arms. Chris was a fine figure of a man. His body had broadened since she had last seen it naked. The boy's figure had gone, this was a man. His face was as wonderful as it had always been, but different now. He was older, wiser. But she recognised the look in his eyes. It was longing.

'That's how you used to look at me,' she said. 'I always knew what you were thinking.'

'Not hard, Jan. When I looked at you I always used to think the same thing.'

'Which was?' she teased.

'That you were the most beautiful woman I had ever seen. And that I wanted to make love to you.'

'That's nice. How did I look at you?'

He considered this. 'You were better at hiding your feelings than I was. Perhaps it comes with being a woman, learning early not to let your face betray your thoughts. But sometimes I caught you looking at me when you thought I wasn't looking back.'

'And?'

'And then I thought I was the luckiest man in the world.'

'Too much talk of looking, not enough action,' she said. She handed him a sponge. 'I want you to wash me. Wash me all over.'

It took a certain amount of rearranging of limbs, of moving bodies. But when they had finished he was sitting behind her and she was lying back between his legs. 'What's that I feel?' she asked mischievously.

'Would you believe me if I told you it was the soap?'

'Certainly not.'

Then he washed her. She felt infinitely languorous as his hands soaped her body and then gently rinsed it. But after a while she felt she needed more. 'My turn now,' she said. 'Just stay there, don't move.'

She climbed quickly out of the bath, wrapped a towel round her. Then she leaned over the bath and washed him as thoroughly as he had washed her. 'Oh, my,' she said, 'my, oh, my.' She stooped to kiss his damp lips. 'Come through when you're ready. But don't be too long. You must be tired.'

Is this brazen hussy really me? she asked herself as she scampered to her bedroom.

It was a warm night, so there was just a sheet on the bed. She pulled it back—and then changed her mind and lay on the outside. She positioned herself carefully, artfully. One leg slightly bent, the foot against the opposite ankle, one arm behind her head. A position of invitation, of longing. You're turning into a real tart, she thought with a grin. But don't you love it?

She had lit just one candle in her bedroom, positioned carefully in front of the mirror. When he entered her bedroom, naked except for the towel round his waist, she saw his body in all its shadowed perfection. And she heard his sharp intake of breath as he saw her.

'Take that towel off,' she said. 'And then there's no need to say anything else.'

He paused, then shook the towel to the floor. She looked at the maleness of him, the obvious great need he had for her, and then turned her head a little. This was all too much.

The bed sagged as he sat down beside her. Now he was in charge, she had done all that she felt she could—what would he do?

She tried to pretend otherwise to herself, but she was anxious—even frightened. Nothing like this had happened to her for six years. Her engagement had been called off—or had slowly subsided. She had realised that there had been no passion between them. She had liked Peter, but no way had he set her feelings on fire. Nothing had compared with her memories of being with Chris. That had been the problem.

She wondered why she was doing this. Why this sudden decision? Perhaps it was something she just had to do. Chris was an important part of her life. This might help sort out how important a part.

He was still sitting on the side of the bed and she wouldn't look at him. He hadn't touched her yet, but he had to make the next move. She shivered with anticipation—and forced herself to relax.

Just one fingertip. She sighed when it touched her. Just one fingertip, which stroked her forehead, slipped down the side of her face and very gently teased her lips. She bit at it, taking it between her lips holding it as if it were something fragile.

Then onwards, infinitely slowly. The side of her neck, pausing to feel the pulse that now hammered there. Onwards again, and now she was breathing more deeply, knew he could detect the rise and fall of her chest.

His finger traced the curve of her breast, tantalisingly stopped a moment and then he touched the firmness of her nipple. So lovely to feel him there—and then he moved to her other breast.

Her body was flooding with warmth, with anticipation. What would he do next?

The bed creaked again, she felt rather than saw his head move across her body and then he took her breast into his mouth. His tongue did sudden urgent things to her and she moaned with pleasure. She couldn't help herself—she took his head, pulled it closer to her body. He kissed her breasts harder, then leaned back.

His words were almost hypnotic. 'No hurry,' she heard him say, 'there's no hurry. You're so beautiful. I want to see, to touch, to taste all of you, you're so beautiful.'

She sighed.

Then he moved downwards, she felt his lips on the delicate curve of her abdomen, kissing, moving onwards, He couldn't intend to— Was he going to…? She gave a small whimper, half fear, half expectation, and reached to clutch his shoulders. To prevent or to urge on, she didn't know.

And then she called aloud at the delicacy of what was happening. Her hips bucked in a passion that couldn't be denied. He was bringing her so much pleasure, and she welcomed him, legs spread wide now, calling his name, fingers gripping him, holding him to her.

But this was going too far. She wanted to give as well as receive. 'Come here,' she murmured. 'Chris, I want you. Come here, come to me.'

He recognised her message, leaned across, and his mouth crashed down on hers in a kiss hard, demanding and passionate. And she returned it, her arms now tight round his neck. She felt his body above her, smelt the maleness of him. She could tell by his heavy breathing, by the beating of his heart against hers, that he needed her much as she now needed him.

Her hands were on his hips. She squeezed then eased him downwards, towards her, towards her giving. He spoke again but his voice was now different. 'Jan, Jan, I've wanted this for so long, wanted you, dreamed of you.'

'Well, I'm yours now,' she whispered, 'and I want you, too.'

And then they were together. For a moment they just lay there, two bodies as close as could be, his maleness and her femininity fitting together as if they were designed for one another. Then he moved—and so did she. It had been too long, and the passion in both of them was demanding a quick release. She marvelled at the way it was so easy, so obvious, yet so good. They moved faster, her rhythm the same as his, her happiness, her ecstasy matching his until they reached a tumultuous climax, both calling aloud.

'You're so good to me,' he mumbled, 'so very good.'

'You're good to me, too. But you must be tired. Sleep.'

He was asleep before she was. But she was perfectly happy. He didn't say he loved me, she thought as she dropped off to sleep. Perhaps that was a good thing.

* * *

She woke early next morning. Gently, she sat up and gazed down on Chris's sleeping face. It was relaxed, and there was a half smile on his lips. She was reminded of how he had looked six years ago. Then his face had been youthful, showing instantly what he had been thinking. It was like that again now. The caution, the wariness that he usually showed had disappeared.

She had never had a chance to sleep all through the night with him before. Now she knew what she had missed. She had enjoyed it so much—she had never realised how peaceful it was to sleep with the warmth of a body next to hers. She had woken in the middle of the night. Her back had been to him, and his arm had been around her, holding her breast. She had snuggled backwards into him and though he didn't wake, that had made it even more wonderful.

But that had been last night and this was the morning. The magic time had gone. She was Community Nurse Jan Fielding again, not Cinderella.

Still, she had the night before. And no matter what, that would be a memory that would stay with her for the rest of her life.

Then another thought. She knew what she wanted now: she wanted Chris. He was still there—and she was going to fight for him!

She managed to creep out of bed without waking him, and made coffee for two, taking one mug upstairs.

'I can smell a wonderful smell,' a voice mumbled. She placed his mug by the bed, dextrously avoided a grasping hand and said, 'I'm going to the bathroom. Your turn in ten minutes.'

Ten minutes for a quick wash and to get dressed. Then she knocked on the bedroom door and shouted, 'Bathroom's free. I'm going to make breakfast. Come down for it when you're ready.'

No way was she going back in the bedroom while he was still in bed!

She made breakfast and set it in the little alcove off her kitchen. Exactly ten minutes later he appeared at the kitchen door. She had half forgotten that the only thing he had with him was his dress clothes. He looked somehow feckless in the dark trousers and open-necked white shirt—and far too attractive.

'No razor,' he said.

She didn't say that the slight darkening of his chin made him even more attractive.

'I'll forgive you. More coffee?'

He came towards her, obviously intending to kiss her. She avoided the kiss, held out another mug of coffee to him. 'Breakfast,' she said. 'There's cereal, toast, or I can do you a fry-up if you want.'

'Toast would be fine, thank you.' He looked at her cautiously. 'We're being serious this morning?'

'Very serious.' She hesitated, then said, 'Just one thing. Last night was so wonderful that I know I'll never forget it. But that was last night. It's over and we don't talk about it now. Possibly not ever.'

'Not ever is a long time. I take it we are going to talk about something, though?'

Last night and this morning, while he had still been asleep, she had glimpsed the old Chris. But this was the new one, calm, reserved, not giving anything away.

'We're going to talk about the future.'

He nodded but said nothing. She turned, dropped bread into the toaster and placed butter and marmalade on the table. Simple domestic tasks made it easier for her to think.

'When you first came back here I asked John what he was playing at, sending for you. I was sure you didn't want to return. He said I needed closure—and perhaps so did you. What happened six years ago was still very much with us both, and we needed to get it settled.'

'I think we've got it settled,' he said. 'Penny helped us.'

'She did, and I'll always be grateful to her. But she left us with another problem. We started like two new lovers and now—well, I don't know how things will progress. But ultimately I need you in or out of my life—but not both.'

'I want to be in your life.'

She shook her head in distress. 'Chris, I've got this dreadful feeling that I'm about to say something that will part us for another six years. Only this time it might be for ever. Please, please, don't answer this question immediately, and *don't* take it as an ultimatum. The last thing I want to do is force you into anything. But...but...if you take this job in Bangladesh...well, I don't see any place there for me. Do you?'

His voice was low. 'I couldn't take you away from this place. It's your home, it's where you are you. I didn't like it here when I came back. But now I'm starting to feel the way you do. I love the mountains, I love the people. And Bangladesh—you need a special sort of mindset to survive there. And that just isn't you.' He sighed. 'But the hospital...I've dreamed about it for years.'

She had forced him to this—she had to make it brutally

obvious to both of them what his choices were. 'So ultimately it's quite simple. You have to choose between me and Bangladesh.'

'Yes,' he said.

CHAPTER NINE

MONDAY morning. Chris put his face round Jan's door, his expression hunted.

'Things are moving faster than I thought,' he said. 'This afternoon I'm going down to London for a week to talk about the hospital. They want my advice as to how to set it up, they think I know more than anyone.'

She managed to keep her voice calm. 'I'll miss you,' she said. 'Does this mean that you've finally made up your mind to take the job?'

He shook his head in frustration. 'No, it does not. I suspect I'll be put under pressure to take it, but I've been under pressure before. Jan, if I decide to move back to Bangladesh, you'll be the first to know.'

'Well, thank you,' she said. She hoped he didn't detect the bitterness in her voice.

He phoned her twice during the week. Just to say hello, just to keep in touch. And she managed to keep her voice calm, be happy for him, bring him up to date with the gossip. And he liked the gossip. It was as if he was now part of the community. He didn't say much about what he was doing, and she had promised herself that she wouldn't ask if he'd made any decision.

He was due to return late on Saturday, and she had invited him to come to supper. On Saturday morning she just didn't know what to do with herself. Again and again she went over her conversations with him. Had she said anything wrong, had she always heard him right? Was she happy with everything? Was anything missing? And always the same, sad conclusion. Things were just as she remembered them. The only thing lacking was her happiness.

In the end she drove out to the loneliest stretch of moors that she knew. She walked straight up the hillside until, sweating, heart thumping, she reached a ridge. There she lay down on the sheep-cropped grass and watched the clouds sailing across the sky.

She thought of Chris. He had once said he preferred the flatlands to this. The man must be mad! But then he had changed. Now he loved the mountains as much as ever.

She thought that perhaps, if he got the job in Bangladesh and asked her to go with him, she would go. But that was stupid! They'd had their talk, they understood each other. They had decided that there was nothing they could do. She had already told him that at times she knew she would hate him because of it. Apparently that didn't stop her loving him, too.

The ground underneath her was wet, and she was getting cold. So she stood and set off down the hillside again. Time to cook for him.

Chris looked tired when he came in late that evening. It had been a long drive and he had come straight to her without going home first.

'Upstairs and have a bath,' she said. 'You'll feel better after it and you'll appreciate my cooking more.'

'I always appreciate your cooking.' He handed her a gift-wrapped parcel. 'Look, I've brought you a little something.'

'I love presents!' She tore open the parcel. Inside was a box of Belgian chocolates. She didn't recognise the name but they looked expensive. She took one and offered him one. One small bite and... 'Chris, these are gorgeous!'

Dark chocolate, not too sweet, so the chocolate flavour came through. And just a hint of some spice that made it seem different, exotic.

'I'll hide these. And I'll have just one a night.'

'I don't think two a night is excessive,' he said.

They ate a quiet tea together, and then she lay in his arms on the couch.

'I don't want you to talk about your London trip,' she said. 'That's your business, and it's one part of your business that I don't want to know about. But I've got something to ask you, if you think you can do it. How long is the longest you can put off giving an answer about going back abroad?'

'I've promised them an answer in exactly four weeks,' he said. 'Four weeks today.'

She turned her head to look up at him, surprised. 'I thought they wanted an answer before then?'

'They did. They do. But I told them that there were personal reasons preventing me from giving them an answer.'

'Personal reasons? What are they?'

'You,' he said. 'Or me. Or, to be exact, us.'

Joy flooded through her body but she tried not to show it. 'Well, I'm glad,' she said. 'Now what I want from you...can you just not talk about it for those four weeks? Tell me your decision just before you phone them?'

'I can do that,' he said.

She didn't know exactly why she wanted to do it. Often over the past few days she had thought of Penny, of her love affair with the dead David, of how she had said that Jan had a second chance. She wanted to take Chris to Penny's, to show her that she was trying with her second chance. And Penny might even tell Chris about her lost love.

'I'd love to call on Penny,' Chris said gravely that afternoon. 'Any particular reason for the visit?'

'Just keeping in touch. She's an old friend of mine.'

'She's been a friend to both of us,' said Chris. 'I'll drive us round this afternoon.'

Jan phoned Penny to ask if it would be convenient for them to call. 'Look forward to seeing you,' Penny said curtly. 'Can't chat now. I'm looking after my bees.'

When they arrived that afternoon, there was no answer when Jan knocked at the front door. That was unlike Penny. She had been kept waiting on so many front doorsteps in her time that she made it a point of honour to answer as quickly as possible.

Jan knocked again, then a third time.

'Perhaps she's out at the back, can't hear us,' said Chris. 'It's a big garden.'

'She was expecting us. Exactly now. But we'll go round to the back to see.'

There was no sign of Penny in the garden. Chris turned to her, frowned. 'I'm going to climb over the wall, see if she's working in the kitchen and can't hear us.'

'Her hearing is fine.' But now Jan was getting anxious and eager for him to look.

He climbed over the wall, walked a few feet and unbolted the back gate to the garden. The two of them walked through swathes of summer-blooming flowers to the little patio that was just outside the kitchen. They peered through the kitchen window. There were three chairs, a table covered with a white cloth, sandwiches, cakes, pies, all arrayed neatly. There was Penny's Welsh dresser, her blue plates carefully displayed in it. There was the Aga, the cupboards, the noticeboard with the neat notes. And sprawled on the stone floor was the apparently lifeless figure of Penny.

For a moment, all Jan could do was stare at the body of her friend. The horror of the scene was too much for her. She couldn't move as Chris tried the back door, which was locked. Unhesitatingly, he lifted his foot and kicked in the lock, and the splintering crash shocked Jan into action. She was a nurse! She followed Chris as he rushed inside.

There was blood in a pool under Penny's head, but it appeared to have stopped flowing. ABC, Jan thought. Airways. Breathing. Circulation. She knelt by Penny's head, facing Chris.

'She's breathing,' he muttered, 'but there's stridor. I don't like that. And a wheeze... I wonder if...'

'Inject her with adrenaline! Quick!' Jan leaped to her feet, looked for Penny's handbag. It had to be here, Penny never moved more than six feet away from her handbag. Ever.

It was sitting on the Welsh dresser. She upended it, tossed its contents onto the table.

'Adrenaline? You means she's—'

'She's suffering from anaphylactic shock. She has an

instant reaction to peanuts, no matter how small the amount. Even peanut dust can set her off, she nearly died from it when she was in her teens. It's here. Pull her skirt up, Chris, I need to get at her thigh.'

Jan had found Penny's store of Epipens. There were four in all—sometimes one injection wasn't enough. She took off the cap of one of the pens, and pressed it against Penny's thigh. The spring-activated needle pushed through the skin to the necessary depth. Jan held the syringe there for the recommended ten seconds and then a couple more. Then she leaned back and sighed.

'I'll phone for the ambulance,' Chris said, and did so. 'I didn't know Penny was so severely allergic.'

'She didn't want people to know. I think she felt that it showed her as being somehow weak. She could forgive weakness in other people but not herself. She's a proud woman.'

'She was nearly a dead one,' said Chris. He felt for the pulse in Penny's neck. 'I think there's an improvement already. And her eyelids are fluttering.' Then he bent to look at the gash on Penny's head. 'This looks nasty but not life-threatening.'

'I'll fetch my bag,' said Jan. 'There's plenty of dressings there.'

She stood, then sat down abruptly on a chair. 'I'm getting a reaction, Chris. I thought I could cope with disasters. But I can't cope with seeing my friends hurt.'

His voice was curt. 'Right now you're a nurse, not a friend. Go and fetch those dressings.'

Angrily she marched to the front door, went down to her car. And when she returned she felt better. Chris was right. Penny needed a nurse, not a friend. She dressed the head wound.

Then they lifted Penny onto her couch and covered her with a blanket. And waited.

Finally Penny came to. 'Stupid,' she said. 'I was stupid. I bought flour from that new shop in town. Girl on the counter told me that they did make cakes containing nuts, but assured me that there was no way any part of a peanut could have got near my flour. Well, she was wrong, and I'll write to the manager to tell him so.'

'You frightened us,' Jan said. 'When we saw you lying on the floor and the blood there...'

'My fault for moving too fast. I tripped over my own feet, must have hit my head when I fell. And I've got the most awful headache now.'

'I think it's only a cut,' Chris said, 'but A and E will want to take a closer look.'

'Of course they will. And they'll want to keep me in overnight, so I can see just how good nurses are these days.'

'I can hear the ambulance,' Jan said. 'We'll come to the hospital with you and—'

'*You* can come. Chris, was it you that made such a mess of my back door?'

'Afraid so,' said Chris with a grin.

'Can you fix it so it's safe again?'

'No problem whatsoever.'

'Good. After that you can come to the hospital and pick Jan up.'

There was a loud knock at the front door, Jan went to let in the paramedics.

Two hours later Chris drove Jan's car into the hospital car park. She was waiting for him, and jumped in at once. 'You carry on driving, if you don't mind,' she said. 'For some reason I feel a bit...frail.'

'How's Penny?'

'She seems to be fine—though she's getting on for being an old woman. There's no point in going to see her, she's asleep.'

'It hit you hard, didn't it?' he asked gently. 'Seeing her lying there like that?'

'I'm used to all sorts of trauma, I'm a nurse. But when it's someone close to you...' She shrugged. 'Perhaps I'm not as tough as I think.'

They drove on in silence for a few minutes and then he asked, apparently casually, 'Was there any special reason for our visit?'

Jan thought of all the things she might say. It would be the good, the noble thing to say nothing. But instead she said, 'Last time I visited her she showed me photographs of the man she loved and had wanted to marry. He died in a motorcycle accident. I thought she might like to tell you about it, too.'

'Poor Penny. But why should she want to tell me about it?'

'To show that you're lucky if you get a second chance.'

Jan leaned forward, shook the front of her dress. Then she shook out her flared skirt. A few errant flakes of confetti floated to the ground of her living room. 'That was a lovely wedding,' she said. 'I really enjoyed it. Did you?'

Chris was sprawled on her couch, his silver tie now undone. 'I did enjoy it,' he confirmed. 'And I loved looking at you in a hat. Did you know that you haven't taken it off since you put it on this morning?'

Jan turned to look at herself in the mirror, adjusted the

wide brim of her straw boater and tightened the scarlet silk band round it. 'Sometimes I like wearing a hat. It's certainly a change from the hood of my anorak.'

'You look lovely in both. And that pink dress is very effective, too.'

'Sometimes Dr Garrett, I think you're turning into a ladies' man. Just give it plenty of practice and another ten years.'

'The only lady I'm interested in knows how I feel already.'

'Of course,' said Jan. To herself she thought, The trouble is, I *don't* know how you feel. Not entirely.

She went on aloud, 'I feel like getting out of wedding mode and into something more relaxing. D'you want to make us some coffee while I change?'

'Coffee coming in five minutes.' He walked to her kitchen.

They had reached this level of intimacy so quickly. They ate together most evenings, in either his or her cottage. They were seen together everywhere and Jan had noted the approving smiles of all sorts of people. At times she shuddered at the thought of what would happen if nothing came of this relationship, if Chris went back to Bangladesh. The kind but pitying looks would be too much to bear!

The coffee was waiting when she came back downstairs in jeans and shirt. She sat by him on the couch and he put his arm round her.

'I've not been to many weddings,' he said. 'Most of my friends from medical school got married while I was abroad. It's come as a bit of a shock to realise how many of them have settled down, even have kids.'

'Do you feel you're missing something?'

'Possibly.' He grinned.

It had been a wonderful, a fairy-tale wedding. The weather

had been kind to them—warm but not too hot for a bride in a full-length white dress and veil. The ceremony had been held in a little village church and the reception at the village hall, so the newly married couple and the congregation had walked from church to reception. There had been a chance to catch up and gossip with old friends. There had been a dance.

She knew Chris had enjoyed it. He had even put up with the not-so-subtle hints and questions from her friends. He had held her hand, escorted her to her seat, made it obvious to all that they were a couple.

Just before the bride had left on her honeymoon she had whispered to Jan, 'I don't want to throw it. How would it be if I just gave you my bouquet? In public?'

'It would be a bit too obvious,' Jan had whispered back. 'You've got a gang of twenty-one-year-old cousins, all eager to follow in your footsteps. Throw the bouquet over your shoulder and let the lucky one catch it.'

'Jan, I just want you to be as happy as I am.'

Now Jan wriggled a bit closer to Chris, took his hand. 'You don't have to go home tonight, do you?'

'Not if I can stay here,' he said.

They were so happy together. She wanted this to go on for ever. But the four weeks were passing. At the end of that time she would know her fate.

As he had promised, Chris said nothing to her about the job. But she knew there had been numerous phone calls from the charity. Sometimes she found him studying documents that he instantly thrust away when he saw her.

She had thought so hard about Chris. Slowly she had come to the realisation that perhaps going back to Bangladesh wasn't the real problem. Rather, it was something he had said after they had walked across the sands of Morecambe Bay. Something about having learned to be self-contained. Jan knew that there was so much love inside him. He just had difficulty in letting it out. But she was going to show him how!

Two weeks of her allowed four weeks had passed, and Jan felt she might be winning. More and more Chris was becoming accustomed to having her as his lover, and she knew how happy she made him. As happy as he made her. She thought, she hoped he would give up the idea of Bangladesh. Of course she knew that someone had to help the people out there. But she wasn't as confident as Chris was that he was the only man for the job. Surely there must be others as good? Surely he had done his part? Or was that selfish of her?

She was still wondering about that when her world crashed around her.

It seemed a silly thing at first. It happened in her wellwoman clinic. First, Mrs Sledmere came in. The lab had sent back the results, and the X-ray had confirmed the diagnosis. Mrs Sledmere indeed had tuberculosis. But it was in its earliest stages, and would be easy to treat and cure. Surprisingly, Mrs Sledmere wasn't too upset. A disease like this gave her a certain amount of attention and she rather liked it.

Then a blushing Alice Plows came in. She wanted advice on contraception. She wasn't sure yet, but she thought she ought to be prepared. Jan complimented her on being sensible, gave her the usual talk on contraceptive techniques and asked Alice to think what might suit her best. 'Come back next week and, if necessary, I'll arrange for you to see the doctor.'

Jan felt happy: this was a job well done. She had a fifteen-minute break now, and sat down with her cup of tea to look through assorted notes.

And then the bombshell fell.

When talking to Alice she had necessarily talked to her about her menstrual cycle. It was part of the talk she gave to everyone asking for contraceptive advice. Plus many of the patients at her well-woman clinic came with problems with periods: one of the challenges of being a woman.

Jan had never had a problem. Since she had started her periods they had been without physical discomfort and came with clockwork regularity. Never more than a day early or late, never one missed. She smiled to herself, knowing she was lucky.

And slowly the smile faded.

She reached for her diary, scrabbled back through it until she saw the discreet little red dot that she entered whenever her period started. Six weeks ago. She was a fortnight late. But she was never late!

Now she thought back over the past few weeks with Chris. He had been good—she knew he had brought protection, had used it conscientiously. They ought to have been safe. But she knew that no contraceptive was ever a hundred per cent safe.

Frantically, she rechecked the dates. At least a fortnight overdue. That meant that—if she was pregnant—the morning-after pill would be no good now.

So. She might be pregnant. She might not be pregnant. These days it was easy enough to discover which, and she could know within the next few minutes since she had a testing kit in her drawer. She opened the drawer—and her intercom bleeped. Her next patient had arrived. Jan gulped, and shut the drawer.

Somehow she managed to get through the rest of her afternoon's work. Then, her fingers trembling, she rang Chris. She knew he had gone to an outlying village to make a call, and Jan was glad that she didn't have to speak to him in person.

Somehow, she made her voice sound more or less normal. 'Chris? I've got an evil headache, I don't know why. But I'm going home and I'm going straight to bed. Do you mind not coming for tea tonight?'

'Of course I don't mind. Are you all right? I want to help. Shall I come round and—?'

'The best help you can be is to stay away. I'm going to be OK, Chris. If I'm not, I'll ring you. See you tomorrow. Bye.'

She rang off, knowing that that had been a highly unsatisfactory call. She had hurt and upset him. Still, she did need time to herself.

She did go to bed, took a cup of tea with her. She closed her curtains—and thought. By her bedside was the pregnancy testing kit.

Just for a second she thought of having a child—her child, Chris's child—the three of them living happily together. Then she put that thought aside. Other things had to come first.

If she took the test and she was not pregnant, there was no problem. She and Chris could continue as they were. He'd decide whether or not he was going to Bangladesh.

But if she *was* pregnant.... Well, she'd have to tell him. Not for herself, but for him—she knew he'd be incandescent with rage if she was pregnant and didn't tell him. He had a right to know. She also knew that neither of them would consider a termination.

If he knew that she was carrying his baby, he'd stay here with her. She knew that as a fact. But he'd also feel that he had been trapped. He wouldn't have made the choice not to go to Bangladesh. It would have been forced on him. In time he might come to resent her and the child for forcing his hand. And he'd be entitled to.

What to do? She couldn't tell him. She buried her face in her pillow and wept.

There was one more thing she had to do. Next morning she left Chris a message on the surgery intercom, asking him if he could come to see her in her room at morning break. He came, carrying two cups of tea.

'How's the headache, Jan?'

She smiled, waved her hand carelessly. 'Practically gone,' she muttered. 'Just one of those things. Chris, it's ten days till you have to make up your mind about Bangladesh.'

He frowned. 'I thought you didn't want to talk about that.'

'I don't. And, Chris, these past few days with you have been some of the happiest in my life. Now, I don't want to influence you, I really don't. I want you to make up your own mind. But I can't go on like this. It's tearing me up inside, the thought that I have—we have—this and it might end. So, please, please, decide what you have to do. But until you do—well, we're back to friends and colleagues again, not lovers. You'd better not come round tonight.'

She'd forgotten how cool, how analytical he could be. 'Something's happened,' he said. 'What?'

'Nothing's happened! This is just the way I've come to

feel. You once told me that you were too self-contained. Well, I'm not self-contained enough. Just…just let's calm things down for a while.'

'This has nothing to do with Bangladesh. Jan, if you're tiring of me, just say so.'

Now the tears flowed. 'Tiring of you? I never could. Nobody could be that self-contained. Chris, just go. I can't do this. We're friends again but that's all.'

He looked at her for a moment, then turned to leave.

That evening Chris sat alone in his cottage. He had cooked himself a scratch meal, eaten it without even noticing what he'd been eating. He had poured himself a whisky, but the glass remained largely untouched. Neither television nor radio could interest him.

He desperately wanted to see Jan. He even thought of walking round towards her cottage. Not calling, of course, but just being nearby might give him some satisfaction.

That was a ridiculous idea. He wasn't a love-struck teenager. Was he?

She had been adamant that she didn't want him to call.

He realised then that he was lonely.

This was quite a new idea for him. For the past few years he'd been able to work and relax on his own. He'd enjoyed company, but he hadn't needed it. Now he was realising what he had missed.

He could get to be self-contained again—he supposed. But now he knew it was a dead end, cutting him off from so much that was wonderful.

What if he decided that he wanted to stay here—and Jan decided that she didn't want him?

Now he knew that he couldn't envisage life without her.

When he had come in he had thrown a pile of mail onto the table. There wouldn't be anything of interest, mostly the massive amount of advertising material that all doctors got. Still, he may as well sort it before it went in the bin.

One letter he'd missed—yet another message from the charity. Surely they weren't wanting even more information? Wearily, he slit open the envelope.

CHAPTER TEN

SOMEHOW Jan worked through the rest of the week. On Friday night it started to rain. Good. Bad weather suited her mood.

She had seen something of Chris—and had been saddened by the set expression on his face. It was a good thing he didn't know how she was feeling—and why.

She was working in her room in the surgery. She had notes to collate, supplies to order, forms to send to the NHS. Just paperwork, but it was better done when there weren't too many people around. That way it got done faster. *And it stopped you thinking about other things,* that mean little voice inside her said.

After she'd been working for an hour there was a knock on the door. It was Chris. He looked at her defensively. 'Working late?' he asked. 'I saw the light and I just thought I'd check.'

She pointed at her desk. 'Finishing my paperwork. What are you doing here?'

'The same, trying to clear my desk. Jan, can we talk about what's wrong?'

'There's nothing wrong. We can talk next week. When you decide about Bangladesh.'

'What if I—?'

She held up her hand. 'Not yet, Chris. Next week.' He hesitated, and she said sharply, 'I mean it.'

He left.

She worked on and the weather got worse. Even in the storm-proofed surgery she could hear the winds moaning and the frames rattling in the windows. At nearly midnight, the phone rang. She was startled enough to jump.

It was Perry, his voice curt. 'Sounds like a bad one, Jan. A small plane has crashed. At least one person known to be alive. It's too dark, too windy for the helicopters, so it's down to us. Going to be a hard rescue.'

'Where's the crash?'

'The east end of Carran Edge. Is Chris with you?'

'I think he's still in the surgery, yes.'

'Let him know he's needed, I've got in touch with all the others. I'm on my way to the surgery. We'll rendezvous there.'

Jan gazed at the telephone. Carran Edge was the ridge her father had died on. She hadn't been there since. Now she was setting off on another rescue—and in similar weather.

Memories from six years ago came crowding back. She couldn't go back there, not on a night like this when...

Quickly she put away her files, grabbed the ever-present sack of walking gear that was never far from her. And as she ran down the corridor, she met Chris.

'You're in a hurry,' he said mildly. 'Is there a crisis?'

'Yes. The rescue team's been turned out, you'd better get changed. Small plane crashed on the top of Carran Edge. Perry's picking us up in five minutes.'

'Carran Edge? The place where...' And then his eyes turned to the nearest window, saw the storm. 'You're going out in this?'

'We're going out in this. You and me and six others. On the ridge where my father died. It'll be the first time I've been on it in six years. But I'm a professional, I can do it. So must you.'

There was no time for more conversation, for personal concerns. They had work to do.

As soon as he was changed he joined her in the storeroom where the mountain rescue kit was kept, and helped her drag it out. A moment later two Land Rovers roared up and the team began loading the kit. Jan climbed into a different vehicle from Chris. And then the two vehicles bumped off into the night.

They arrived at the field where they would leave their vehicles and started to pull out all their kit. And when they had unloaded it, heaved on their rucksacks, checked that their lights were working, that nothing had been left behind—then it was time to go.

She gazed into the darkness ahead of them. Behind her, a gentle voice asked, 'Are you nervous? Because I am.'

'I'm not sure what we're doing here. This trip is turning into more than a rescue mission. We're working together again, almost exactly six years since the last time we were here. It feels like a search for two people's lost souls.'

They set off up the steep slope, Jan and Chris bringing up the rear. This time there was no surreptitious holding of hands, no quick kissing of rainswept faces, as there had been before. Apart from anything else they needed all their breath to keep up the cracking pace that Perry was setting, but it was possible to gasp out a few words.

'What are you thinking?' she asked him.

'Probably the same as you,' came the sombre reply. 'I

don't want to do this. But there's someone up there who might need our help. So we stop thinking about ourselves and think about someone else.'

'Can you stop thinking about us? Because I can't.'

'Neither can I,' came the reluctant reply.

After that there was nothing to say. If anything, the storm got worse. The wind howled straight towards them; they had difficulty in standing upright, had to flounder from foothold to foothold. And even in the dark she saw boulders, runs of stone, that she remembered from six years before. Chris didn't even turn his head. Perhaps a good thing. She decided to try not to think about it herself.

Another hour's ankle-turning walking, and then Perry called a short halt. They grouped in the lee of a giant rock as he listened to a message coming through from John Garrett, who had come to act as co-ordinator in the surgery below.

'John's just asked for our ETA,' Perry shouted. 'I've had to tell him we're not doing very well, that conditions are dreadful. He says they've had a message from the wrecked plane. It sounds as if one of the passengers has got a tension pneumothorax. And if someone medically competent doesn't get to him in the next half-hour, he's going to die.'

'Half an hour?' one of the team said. 'No. Just not possible. An hour is the earliest.' The others nodded agreement.

Jan heard someone laugh behind her. Not an ordinary, humour-filled laugh, but a laugh at the cruel jokes that fate could play on people. It was Chris.

'There is a quicker way to the plane,' he said. 'In fact, I've done it before. You go along Pitt's Rake and then climb fifty feet up the face at the end. And you're only a couple of hundred yards from the crash.'

'No.' Perry's voice was decisive. 'I'm in charge. We don't risk a team member's life any more than we have to. And the last time you went along Pitt's Rake—'

'The last time I went along Pitt's Rake, the man with me died,' said Chris. 'As you all know, he was Jan's father. And I've spent six years wondering if there was anything different I should have done. But that's by the way. As we talk we're risking a man's life. I want to take the fast way, try to save him.'

'And I'll go with you,' said Jan.

'You won't,' snapped Chris. 'I don't want you, I don't need you.'

'You might not want me. You will need me.'

There was silence for a couple of seconds and then Perry said, 'I'm going to have words with you two when this operation is over. I may kick you both out of the team. We don't squabble when we need to be united. But I'm making a decision now. Both of you go along Pitt's Rake. Do what you can. And good luck. The rest of you, let's get moving.'

'We'd better move, too,' Jan said, and moved to where she knew the beginning of Pitt's Rake ran along the slide of a sheer cliff.

Chris grabbed her arm. 'How'd you think I'll feel if you get killed?' he yelled.

'You'll feel exactly as I'd feel if you got killed. My life would be pointless. Now, can we get on with the operation and stop arguing? The path's that way.'

'I know the way and I'll lead,' he growled. 'But first we rope together.' And then they set off.

It was a perilous traverse. Sometimes they had to cling to the rock and inch forward on their hands and knees. The wind buffeted them. The rain scratched at the little of their faces that were exposed. But they made progress. And eventually they came to the face at the end of the Rake.

Fifty feet of sheer rock. Not too difficult in daylight, when there was no wind. Not too easy on a windy night.

'This is where your father fell,' Chris shouted into Jan's ear. 'Now, I want no argument. I take the rope, climb first. You're my second. Got that?'

She could give him that much. 'Sounds good to me,' she yelled back.

It was odd, watching him climb. After a while his body disappeared into the darkness and all she could see was the bright yellow disc of his torch as the beam flickered across the wet rock. She saw him hesitate, retreat a couple feet, before taking a new route. But finally he was up. And she heard his screamed order. 'Belayed! Start climbing!'

It was harder than anything she had ever done. But she seemed to be making good progress until she placed a hand on a hold that wasn't quite there. Then she lurched backwards, the other hand and both feet peeled from the rock, and after a short but terrifying drop—no more than three feet—the rope round her waist tightened and she stopped with a stomach-heaving jerk.

'I've got you! You OK?' came the shouted words.

'I'm fine and I'm moving.' She scrabbled her way back onto the rock and started to climb again. Five minutes later Chris grabbed the neck of her anorak and heaved her over the edge. 'We've made it. Look, the plane's over there. Let's hope we're not too late.'

Some distance away they could see dim lights.

They were on the mountain summit now. The ridge flattened out here, and there was a small flat piece of boggy land. As they walked nearer the lights they saw that they came from inside the crashed plane. A possible sign of life.

The pilot had been incredibly skilful or incredibly lucky. He had found the only patch of flat land on the entire range. But he hadn't managed to land properly. The tail of the aircraft was up in the air, one wing had been torn off and the engine was buried in the boggy ground.

They walked towards the plane, stopped a distance from it. 'Wait here a minute,' Chris said. 'I'll do the prelim check. But I'll do it fast.'

That was protocol. Any crashed vehicle was approached carefully by one man, assessed for danger to the rescue team.

Chris approached the plane, cautiously walked round it then moved forward to peer into the cabin. Only then did he wave for her to come closer.

There had been four men in the plane. Triage. Who needed to be treated first? The two of them peered through the smashed windows.

The pilot was silent. The man sitting by his side had his eyes closed but was moaning and breathing noisily—apparently without getting too much oxygen. In the back there were two men—one apparently unconscious, his face covered with blood but with a rough bandage round it. The other man looked up as they approached.

'Thank God you've got here,' he said. 'I've been waiting and wondering. But you're here now and I can... Well, I did what I could for Arthur here and I phoned you and...'

He was showing signs of confusion, and they could see his pallor and the perspiration on his face. 'Probably shock,'

Chris muttered to Jan. To the man he said, 'Who was having difficulty breathing?'

'It was Mickey. Mickey in the front there. I did what I could for him and I talked to the doctor on the radio, but he wanted me to stick something in Mickey's chest and let the air out, and—'

'Don't worry,' Jan soothed. 'We'll see to it. Just lie back and try to rest. You'll feel better soon.'

'What do you think of this, Jan?' Chris had opened Mickey's shirt and jacket. 'I don't like his breathing.'

The signs were obvious to an experienced eye. A fast respiratory rate, fast, weak pulse, less air entry to the hemithorax, a deviated trachea. Patient losing consciousness, unable to communicate but in considerable discomfort. This was a tension pneumothorax. John had been clever to diagnose it.

A lung had been punctured and air was leaking into the pleural cavity. In time it could cause the lung to collapse.

'There's no way we can do a chest drain up here,' Chris said. 'All we can do is decompress the chest by getting a venflon cannula into the pleural cavity. We'll let the ambulance team know that they need a medical team to get a drain in as soon as possible.'

Jan nodded, looked through her kit to find a cannula and ten-mil syringe. She cleaned the skin and then watched as Chris inserted the cannula, heard the hiss of air as the air in the lung escaped.

'He's got a better chance now,' Chris said. 'We've done all we can for the moment. Now triage. What else have we got?'

The pilot was sitting next to Mickey, who was now more comfortable as he was able to breathe properly. Chris felt the pilot's neck for a pulse. Then he shook his head at Jan. 'Poor devil's got a broken neck and multiple skull fractures. I'm pronouncing him dead.'

It was always best if a doctor could pronounce death at a scene. It meant that the hospital staff didn't have to go through the unpleasant procedure of pretending that the man might be alive and trying unnecessary resuscitation.

Jan was still comforting the shocked man, telling him that everything was all right, feeding him a warm, sweet drink. She took his pulse. It was getting stronger as the man felt warm, comfortable, less frightened.

'Just lie here,' Jan said. 'We're all around you, you're going to be all right.'

'What about the others? I bandaged Martin, but there was nothing I could do for the pilot and I…'

'You did really well. Now stop worrying. Everything is going to be all right.'

Chris had managed to climb inside the plane and was making a swift assessment of the one remaining passenger. Then he climbed out again, rummaged through his rucksack. 'I think we know what's wrong. He's bleeding badly, but we can bandage him and get some fluids into him. I suspect a fractured skull, concussion. A low Glasgow coma score. He hit his head on the side of the plane when it crashed. All we can do up here is keep his fluids up, check his breathing and airway regularly.'

'How's his neck?'

Chris held up what he had been looking for in the rucksack. A hard collar. 'I suspect his neck is fine. But we'll get this on him.'

'We're here. What can we do?' A shout from outside the

plane. Jan peered at a set of figures. The rest of the team had arrived.

'There's some clearing up to do here,' Chris said, 'then it's a long, hard trek down. Three people need stretchers.'

'Only three?'

'I've pronounced the pilot dead. We'll cover him, leave him in the plane. There's nothing more we can do for him.'

Three people to carry on stretchers, eight people to carry them. It was going to be a hard journey down. But perhaps the weather was easing a little. Jan thought so. Or was it just the relief of having managed so much?

Perry got back in touch with John, reported what they had found, what they had done, what they were doing. Then he looked up and gave a tired grin. 'Not as hard as we expected. John's found a set of RAF squaddies on a leadership course. They're sending ten of them up to meet us to help with the stretchers.'

'This is our rescue!' someone shouted.

Perry shook his head, pointed at the three stretchers now completely assembled. 'No,' he said, 'it's theirs.'

Time to set off back. Their progress would be slower. They had three extra heavy loads to carry and, as far as possible, those loads had to be handled gently. But moving over rough ground, carrying stretchers with injured people strapped in, ignoring the weather—that was something they had practised, were expert at. Move with all possible speed. But never hurry, never risk dropping a patient.

Returning along the ridge was hard. It was not just a case of two or four men carrying a simple load. Sometimes the entire team had to manhandle a stretcher down a rocky stretch or through knee-deep mud. But they managed. And when they started down the hillside, the going was faster and the weather seemed a little less hostile.

Jan knew she was fit, strong, and she was trained for this kind of work. But never had she been more pleased than when she saw a group of lights coming towards them and knew that trained, fresh men were approaching who could take over. Her arms felt like they had been pulled out of their sockets.

'We can take it easy now,' she gasped to Chris.

'Easier perhaps,' he said. 'But those three are still our patients. We see them to safety, only hand them over to equally competent medical care.'

In fact, they were to be relieved completely. The RAF team included a doctor and three paramedics, all specifically trained for outdoor emergencies. Chris gave a quick report on each man then happily handed over responsibility. The weary rescue team stood by and watched as the RAF personnel carried their rescued men down the hillside at what seemed an alarmingly fast speed.

'D'you think they could carry a couple of us down as well?' one of the team asked.

They were still a fair way up the side of the mountain, but the sense of urgency had left them. It seemed as if their purpose had been taken away—as it had—and they rather regretted it.

The path was still steep and the wind blew even more strongly, and it was an effort to take every step. Jan had walked in this kind of weather before, but it still needed all her strength. They walked in single file, hunched against the driving rain, staggering whenever a squall hit them.

She was tired and perhaps she got careless. And that meant it was almost certain to happen. She had forgotten that most mountain accidents took place in the last hour of a trip.

She was stepping down the smooth face of a boulder, the far side of a split in the rocks. It was called Cole's Leap. If it was dry and the weather fine, climbers would jump it, ignoring the twenty-foot drop below. On their way up they had stood in line and helped each other stride across.

The wind gusted, caught her off balance and she slipped.

Chris was just behind her. He grabbed her, tried to steady her, but the wind was too much for them. For a moment they teetered there, about to fall down the split. Then he jerked himself backwards, pulling her with him so she fell on top of him. His body was a cushion for hers, and she hit him hard. But they were both safe.

The group stopped, lights focussed on the pair of them. Jan took the necessary minute to check all was well—stretched arms, legs, neck, carefully wriggled her back. It was always a good thing, after a fall onto hard ground, not to move at once. However, she hadn't fallen onto hard ground, she'd fallen onto Chris. Quickly, she climbed to her feet. Chris lay there a second. The lights showed his face twisted in pain.

It was Perry who asked. 'You all right, Chris?'

'Bruised a bit, but I'll live.' He took Perry's outstretched hand, climbed painfully to his feet. 'Let's move,' he said. Much more careful now, they stepped across Cole's Leap. And then they moved.

'It's no good being a hero,' Jan said to Chris after a while. 'If you're hurt, now is the time to say so. We've got a spare stretcher, we can make you comfortable and carry you the rest of the way. If you collapse on us now, you'll cause much more trouble.'

'I'm OK! Just a bit stiff. Jan, I'm a doctor. I'll know if anything is wrong.'

'A man who diagnoses himself has a fool for a doctor,' she muttered. But she decided to say nothing more.

Finally they reached their Land Rovers. It was five in the morning. The rescue team stood for a minute in the rain and the dark. Jan knew what they felt. For the past few hours all their endeavours, all their thoughts and strength had been focussed to one end. Usually this was the time that they handed over their charges, briefed the paramedics as to what treatment they had given, what observations they had made. It was a time of modest self-congratulation. But the RAF and the ambulance were long gone. Now their purpose had gone and, as well as being exhausted, they were a little lost.

'Good job, well done,' Perry said. 'We'll get together, talk about it later in the week. But now let's get everyone to bed.'

They drove back to the surgery to dump their kit. Jan and Chris got out there, too, watched the two Land Rovers drive away. 'Want a lift back to your cottage?' Chris asked. 'Then I could pick you up in the morning to fetch your car.'

'You can drive me back to my cottage. And then you're staying the night. I've got things to say to you.'

'Perhaps we've got things to say to each other.'

CHAPTER ELEVEN

IT WASN'T to be like the previous nights they had spent together, nights of expectation and passion. This time both were cold, wet and exhausted.

'Up to the bathroom,' she said. 'You can undress there and I'm going to help you.'

'Very nice, too,' he said.

'I'm going to help you because for the moment I'm your nurse, not your lover. I want to see your naked body, not because I'm attracted to it, but because I think it's damaged. Now, upstairs.'

'You'd make a great hospital matron,' he said. 'One of the old kind.' But Chris went upstairs, and as she followed him she saw how slowly he was moving.

Not a bath, she thought, but a shower. It might be a good idea not to have him bending too much. Jan left him to undress, telling him to throw his sodden clothes into the basket. Then she went to her bedroom, stripped off her own clothes and wrapped a dressing-gown around her.

He was standing in her bathroom, a towel round his waist, trying to look over his shoulder at his reflection in the mirror. Jan felt a flash of excitement—then winced as she saw what he was trying to see. Down one side of his back there was a great red weal. Red at the moment, but she knew that by morning it would be black. He was terribly bruised.

'You got that bruise when I fell,' she said. 'And you deliberately twisted so that you'd be under me. You wanted to save me.'

He shrugged. 'We both fell. I don't remember any twisting.'

She decided not to argue. Instead, she turned him so the light shone on his back. Gently, she ran her fingers down the great red mark. 'Bruising is pretty bad, but it'll pass. What's the chances of you having broken a rib?'

As she spoke she felt for the bones under the skin, tried to feel if there was any break or crack.

'I don't think so. If I had, then when I twist my body there should be some extra pain.' Slowly, he twisted. She could tell that it hurt him—but after a while, when he straightened, he seemed a little relieved. 'No really sharp pain. I think my ribs are intact.'

'Could you have damaged a kidney?'

He grinned at her. 'No blood in my urine, Nurse. I checked while you were out of the room.'

'Well, I'd still be happier if you went to A and E. But as it is we'll wait till morning. Now, I think a shower rather than a bath. It'll mean you have to do much less bending.'

'No bending? That'll be difficult. I need to…'

'You don't need to anything. I'm getting in the shower with you, I'll wash you. And that is so we can both get clean and warm and dry. Not for any other reason.'

'What other reason could there possibly be?'

'Just drop the towel, Garrett.'

She turned on the shower, adjusted the settings. When

she'd had her cottage rebuilt, one of her priorities had been a large, comfortable bathroom. And there was plenty of room for two in her shower cabinet.

He seemed hesitant. How could he be, the man who had made love to her—with her—not so long ago? The man who had seen her naked, been naked with her, who had rejoiced in it? Perhaps it was because they were now nurse and patient. She'd have to show him.

She slipped out of her dressing-gown, reached for the knot on his towel. Then she took him by the hand and led him into the cabinet. The warm water hissed down over them both and it was very relaxing. For a moment they just stood there, she holding his arms. The water beat on his head, flattening the thick dark hair and mysteriously making his blue eyes seem clearer than ever. And the message the eyes gave out was even clearer. Jan shook herself, reminded herself that she was a nurse. Sort of.

'There's no way I'm going to let a sweaty, dirty man into my nice clean bed,' she said. 'So just stand there and I'll make you presentable.'

He stood there. She dripped shampoo onto his hair, rubbed at the suds and watched them as the water coursed white down his body. He was taller than her, so she had to stand close to him, holding up her arms. The tips of her breasts just touched his chest.

'That...is...very nice,' he said, his voice hoarse.

'Just a shampoo.' What else?

He reached for the soap, but she took it from him. 'I don't want you bending any more,' she said. 'Just keep perfectly still.' And she washed his face, his arms, his chest. Then she had to kneel.

'Perhaps I can...' he started, if anything, his voice even more hoarse.

'You can't bend. Chris, I'm a nurse, I've washed no end of male patients in my time. It's just a job. With you it might be a pleasant job. But a job is all it is.'

She wondered who she thought she was kidding.

'You've never washed a patient kneeling in a shower cabinet!'

'Now, that is true,' she admitted. 'But the aim is the same. All I'm doing is getting you clean.' But she had to admit to herself that that bit wasn't quite true either.

Finally, she was finished. She took him by the hand, led him out of the cabinet. Then she dabbed him dry and led him to her bed. 'I'll fetch you some tea and then get washed myself,' she told him. 'And then there's just one thing I want to say to you.'

'Jan, we have to—'

'Just rest.' She fetched two mugs of tea, and added a healthy shot of whisky to them. Then she quickly had her own shower, put on a long nightie and scampered back to climb into bed with Chris.

She reached for her mug of tea. 'Things have changed,' she said. 'Earlier tonight I slipped on Cole's Leap. I could have been killed but you saved me. There's nothing like the prospect of death to concentrate the mind.'

She leaned over, kissed him gently on the lips. 'Tomorrow is Saturday, we have all day,' she said. 'But now I'm tired and we can talk in the morning.'

'Talk...or something,' he said.

But next morning *something* wasn't really possible. When they woke he put his arm round her head and tried to lean to kiss her. Her eyes were open and she saw the pain flash across his face.

'Your back's worse,' she said.

'Just ordinary bruising and stiffening up. When I move it hurts a bit.'

'Seems to me that it hurts a lot. Just what did you have in mind?'

'Well,' he said. 'What I thought was, what I'd really like for us to do is…'

'You can't, not with a badly bruised back.' Jan smiled, leaned forward and kissed him quickly on the forehead. 'But Nurse Jan Fielding has a solution.'

She pulled her nightie over her head, threw it to the end of the bedroom. Then she knelt across him. 'You can't move,' she said, 'but I can. I think I've spent too long not making decisions. I'm changing all that. I'm going for what I want.'

'Jan…this is…this is…'

She bent down to kiss him. 'This is wonderful,' she said. 'I feel I've got you all—yes, all of you. Now you may hold my breasts if you wish. And be happy, because I'm going to be.'

Some time later she lay by his side, her head on his shoulder, her arm round his waist. 'I'm very upset,' she said, in a not very upset voice. 'I know now what I've been missing. Will I ever make it up?'

'We could start trying now,' he offered. But she guessed it was just bravado.

After a moment they both spoke together.

'Jan, there's something I've got to—'
'Chris, there's something you should—'

They both laughed. 'Is yours good news?' she asked.

'I think so. I desperately hope so. I've been wanting to tell you but you seemed a bit…'

'I was. I've been rotten to you and I'm sorry. What have you got to tell me?'

'The government in Bangladesh has insisted that the director of the new hospital be a native of the country, and the charity has agreed. They're very sorry but I'm not wanted as director. But if I'm wanted here…'

'Oh, Chris! Then you can stay!' She couldn't help herself. She threw herself onto him—and then blanched as she heard his hiss of pain. 'Sweetheart, I've hurt you!'

'It doesn't matter. What matters is that you want me to stay.' He tightened his arm round her. 'Now tell me what's been wrong for the past few days.'

'I'm not sure this is going to be exactly good news,' she said. 'And so far nothing is certain. But it could be good news.'

'Nurse Fielding! You're starting to aggravate me!'

'Sorry, Dr Garrett,' she said demurely. 'Perhaps it'll be better if I demonstrate rather than tell you. I've got this ready to use.' From her bedside cabinet she took the pregnancy testing kit.

He looked at it, amazed. 'Pregnant? You? How could you be? I've always been careful. I thought that—'

'No contraceptive technique is ever better than ninety-nine point nine per cent effective,' she said. 'That means that someone gets to be the point one per cent failure. I don't know, it's just that usually my periods are very regular. And I'm about a fortnight overdue.'

For a moment he was a doctor, not a lover. 'Not really significant,' he said. 'Periods can be erratic for all sorts of reasons, you know that.' Then he became a lover again. 'Why haven't you used the test?'

She wondered how he'd take this. 'I thought if I was pregnant I'd have to tell you. And you'd feel trapped.'

'Never. Never, never, never. You should have known me better than that. Jan, there's something I've never told you.'

'There is?' she asked cautiously.

'There is. Jan Fielding, I love you.'

She thought about the words. They sounded so good, she'd try them herself. 'And I love you, Chris Garrett,' she said. 'Would you like to kiss me?'

He would, and he did.

She relaxed in his arms, relishing the warm glow of happiness. 'It feels like my day has just had a new sunny dawn.'

As if to prove her wrong, rain suddenly spattered on the window. 'Typical Lakeland weather,' she said.

'I like the weather. Jan, my uncle has offered me a partnership. I think I'll accept. Stop roving, settle down. Settle down with you.' He sat up. 'Will you marry me? It's taken me a while to realise it—but no one could love you more than I do.'

She sat up too and kissed him. 'Of course I'll marry you. And we'll be the happiest couple anywhere.'

She reached over to take the package from him. 'Now, shall I go and see if you're going to be a father?'

'Well, I'm quite curious,' he said. 'Why not?'

Extra medical drama for your money!

MILLS & BOON

Medical romance™

Extra

Maggie Kingsley and Laura Iding

3 stories set in the exciting world of A&E

Where passions run high and love and lives are on the line!

Emergency: Love

On sale from 4th August 2006

Available at most branches of WHSmith, Tesco, ASDA, Borders, Eason, Sainsbury's and most bookshops

Visit www.millsandboon.co.uk

0706/03a

MILLS & BOON
Live the emotion

Medical romance™

THE SICILIAN DOCTOR'S PROPOSAL
by Sarah Morgan

Mediterranean Doctors
Passionate about life, love and medicine.

Dr Alice Anderson doesn't believe in love – no matter how much the new doctor Dr Giovanni Moretti tries to persuade her otherwise. Gio's feelings for Alice are undeniably strong. But will the impossibly charming Sicilian be able to make Alice realise that she has done the unthinkable – fallen in love?

THE FIREFIGHTER'S FIANCÉ *by Kate Hardy*

Kelsey Watson loves her firefighting job, is happily single and she has a wonderful friend and housemate in paramedic Matt Fraser. Then Matt notices how deeply a fierce fire in a local school affects Kelsey. And as he tries to help her, a deeper connection between them emerges…

EMERGENCY BABY *by Alison Roberts*

As part of the Specialist Emergency Response Team, paramedic Samantha Moore has always been one of the boys. But now her biological clock is ticking – and she wants a baby! Sam begins to search for the perfect father…and discovers him right under her nose: her SERT partner, Alex! Soon Sam begins to see Alex as the perfect husband too.

On sale 4th August 2006

Available at WHSmith, Tesco, ASDA, Borders, Eason, Sainsbury's and most bookshops

www.millsandboon.co.uk

MILLS & BOON

Live the emotion

Medical romance™

BRIDE AT BAY HOSPITAL by Meredith Webber

Bad boy Sam Agostini left the bay thirteen years ago, leaving Nurse Megan Anstey broken-hearted. Now he is back, still devastatingly handsome, still undeniably charming, and a highly respected doctor. As Sam fights to make up to Megan for his past, new secrets start to bubble to the surface...

THE FLIGHT DOCTOR'S ENGAGEMENT
by Laura Iding

*Air Rescue:
High flying doctors – High altitude medical drama*

Flight doctor Zach Taylor is intrigued by his partner – fiery paramedic Jenna Reed. There is more to Jenna than meets the eye – and he is intrigued by her determination to rescue everyone and everything. Zach can see that it's Jenna herself who needs saving – his plan is to do exactly that and, hopefully, also win her heart!

IN HIS SPECIAL CARE by Lucy Clark

Despite being Mt Black Hospital's only full-time GP, Dr Claire Neilson always finds time for her patients. But Claire doesn't let anyone care for her...until the new specialist – incredibly handsome, enigmatic Dr Declan Silvermark arrives in the small Australian town and turns her carefully ordered world upside down...

On sale 4th August 2006

Available at WHSmith, Tesco, ASDA, Borders, Eason, Sainsbury's and most bookshops

www.millsandboon.co.uk

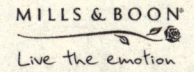

THE SERIES YOU LOVE IS GETTING EVEN BETTER

This September, Tender Romance™ is getting a new look and improving on the stories you know and love.

Tender Romance is becoming *Mills & Boon® Romance.* You'll find your favourite authors and more of the stories you love— we're just making them better!

Watch for the new, improved Mills & Boon Romance series at your favourite bookseller this autumn.

MILLS & BOON®

Romance
Pure romance, pure emotion

4 FREE

BOOKS AND A SURPRISE GIFT!

We would like to take this opportunity to thank you for reading this Mills & Boon® book by offering you the chance to take FOUR more specially selected titles from the Medical Romance™ series absolutely FREE! We're also making this offer to introduce you to the benefits of the Reader Service™—

- ★ **FREE home delivery**
- ★ **FREE gifts and competitions**
- ★ **FREE monthly Newsletter**
- ★ **Exclusive Reader Service offers**
- ★ **Books available before they're in the shops**

Accepting these FREE books and gift places you under no obligation to buy, you may cancel at any time, even after receiving your free shipment. Simply complete your details below and return the entire page to the address below. You don't even need a stamp!

YES! Please send me 4 free Medical Romance books and a surprise gift. I understand that unless you hear from me, I will receive 6 superb new titles every month for just £2.80 each, postage and packing free. I am under no obligation to purchase any books and may cancel my subscription at any time. The free books and gift will be mine to keep in any case.

M6ZED

Ms/Mrs/Miss/Mr .... Initials ....

BLOCK CAPITALS PLEASE

Surname ....

Address ....

....

.... Postcode ....

Send this whole page to:
UK: FREEPOST CN81, Croydon, CR9 3WZ

Offer valid in UK only and is not available to current Reader service subscribers to this series. Overseas and Eire please write for details. We reserve the right to refuse an application and applicants must be aged 18 years or over. Only one application per household. Terms and prices subject to change without notice. Offer expires 31st October 2006. As a result of this application, you may receive offers from Harlequin Mills & Boon and other carefully selected companies. If you would prefer not to share in this opportunity please write to The Data Manager, PO Box 676, Richmond, TW9 1WU.

Mills & Boon® is a registered trademark owned by Harlequin Mills & Boon Limited.
Medical Romance™ is being used as a trademark. The Reader Service™ is being used as a trademark.

MILLS & BOON

Live the emotion

0706/05b

Their Secret Child

3 Full-length novels ONLY £4.99

Featuring
The Latin Lover's Secret Child by Jane Porter
Her Baby Secret by Kim Lawrence
The Greek Tycoon's Secret Child
by Cathy Williams

Make sure you buy these irresistible stories!

On sale 4th August 2006

Available at WHSmith, Tesco, ASDA, Borders, Eason,
Sainsbury's and most bookshops

www.millsandboon.co.uk

0706/05a

MILLS & BOON

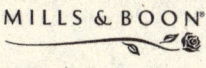

Live the emotion

In August 2006 Mills & Boon bring back two of their classic collections, each featuring three favourite romances by our bestselling authors...

The Counts of Calvani
by Lucy Gordon

Featuring
The Venetian Playboy's Bride
The Italian Millionaire's Marriage
The Tuscan Tycoon's Wife

Make sure you buy these irresistible stories!

On sale 4th August 2006

Available at WHSmith, Tesco, ASDA, Borders, Eason, Sainsbury's and most bookshops

www.millsandboon.co.uk

The child she loves…is his child.

And now he knows…

THE SEVEN YEAR SECRET BY ROZ DENNY FOX

Mallory Forester's daughter needs a transplant. But there's only one person left to turn to – Liddy's father. Mallory hasn't seen Connor in seven years, and now she has to tell him he's a father…with a chance to save his daughter's life!

HIS DADDY'S EYES BY DEBRA SALONEN

Judge Lawrence Bishop spent a weekend in the arms of a sexy stranger two years ago and he's been looking for her ever since. He discovers she's dead, but *her baby son* is living with his aunt, Sara Carsten. Ren does the maths and realises he's got to see pretty Sara, talk to her and go from there…

Look for more *Little Secrets* coming in August!

On sale 7th July 2006

www.millsandboon.co.uk